Whackadoodle Times Three

Also By Kim Antieau

Novels

The Blue Tail • *Broken Moon* • *Butch*
Church of the Old Mermaids • *Coyote Cowgirl*
Deathmark • *The Desert Siren* • *The Fish Wife*
The Gaia Websters • *Her Frozen Wild*
Jewelweed Station • *The Jigsaw Woman*
Killing Beauty • *Mercy, Unbound*
The Monster's Daughter
Queendom: Feast of the Saints
Ruby's Imagine • *Swans in Winter* • *The Rift*
Whackadoodle Times • *Whackadoodle Times Two*

Nonfiction

Answering the Creative Call • *Certified*
Counting on Wildflowers
*Kim and Mario Build a Labyrinth
and So Can You* (with Mario Milosevic)
The Old Mermaids Book of Days and Nights
*The Old Mermaids Book of Days and Nights: A Year
and a Day Journal*
An Old Mermaid Journal
The Old Mermaids Mystery School
The Salmon Mysteries
Under the Tucson Moon

Short Story Collections

Entangled Realities (with Mario Milosevic)
The First Book of Old Mermaids Tales
Haunted
Tales Fabulous and Fairy
Trudging to Eden

WHACKADOODLE TIMES THREE

KIM ANTIEAU

Green Snake
PUBLISHING

For Mario

CHAPTER ONE

I know precisely when things went whackadoodle again. Eartha did not show up on my doorstep offering perfect margaritas. No fake robbers burst into the restaurant where I was breakfasting with my blackmailing daughter. Nope. It was a perfect February day in the canyon at my old house. They were all sitting outside enjoying the sun, and I was cleaning up after the dinner party. I picked up a wine glass on the counter that had a splash or two of white wine sloshing in the bottom of it. Instead of tossing the wine into the sink and putting the glass in the dishwasher, I brought the glass up to my lips, breathed deeply the scent of fermenting grapes, leaned my head back, then drained the wine into my mouth.

I didn't swallow right away. I waited a beat. A nanosecond. An eon.

Then I swallowed.

It tasted like Nirvana.

If Nirvana was a place where addicts went to drink warm white wine that tasted vaguely of someone else's lipstick.

Addicts always have an excuse for relapsing. My excuses could have been that the biosphere was crashing and burning, I believed Mark and I were finished once and for all again, my first son David would turn 17 soon and his anxiety was still full-blown, and my second son Alberto would be a teen now if he had lived.

Or my excuse could have been that my ex-husband Hayword had arranged this dinner party so we could all meet his new girl-friend Patricia who was now listening with rapt attention to my son talk about climate change like she was his new momma come calling. David kept talking about some strange lightning storm coming this week that they were predicting could kill us all. And p.s. Hayword isn't really my ex-husband. We have not officially divorced. Still.

Or maybe my excuse could have been that I was late delivering the screenplay for *Beauty and the Zombie Part Three: Whackadoodle Times.* Sally St. James kept telling me that the fate of our entire studio rested on my shoulders. Again.

But I ain't gonna make any excuses. Even though any one of those would have been good ones. The truth is I swallowed that wine because that's what a drunk does. Even one who has been sober for five years.

Give me some credit though. I didn't pick up another half-ass half-filled glass of wine or start desperately rummaging through the cupboards looking for liquor. I stood in the kitchen breathing, leaning against the white cupboards, my hands on the wooden countertops, my fingers holding on to the edge for dear life.

I could hear them outside laughing and talking: David, Hayword, dearest wanna-be-momma Patricia, and my best friend Joanie. My daughter Fern was off somewhere. She had stopped by the bungalow a couple days ago when I wasn't home. She left me a note on the kitchen countertop, next to a bottle of Martinelli's sparkling apple cider (already opened) and a piece of cherry pie from Nellie's. Two of my favorite things to consume. She had sounded fine in the note.

In fact, my whole family seemed fine without me. I breathed. What a relief. What a relief. What a fucking relief. They were fine without me.

What we had all feared had come to pass: I had taken another drink.

And the world had not ended.

"What are you doing in here?" Joanie asked, suddenly in the kitchen, suddenly beside me, opening up the refrigerator with the hand that wasn't holding a drink.

"I'm cleaning up," I said. I let go of the countertop and began putting dishes in the dishwasher once again.

Joanie closed the fridge and picked up one half-empty wine glass after another and gulped down the contents before handing me each glass. "See," she said, grinning. "I'm helping, too."

I didn't say anything. I could hear my heart beating in my ears. Or was that the alcohol pulsing through my veins, singing, "More, more, more?"

Joanie stood too close to me. She was always too close. She had no sense of personal space. Never had. Sometimes that made me love her all the more. Now, I could smell the alcohol on her. Not on her breath. Was she sweating it?

"Are you doing anything to prepare for this lightning storm?" Joanie asked. "They say we should all stay indoors once it starts and stay until it ends. Will it burn down our houses? Will our phones die?"

"Why are you asking me? Do I look like a weather vane?"

"They say that just before, during, and after a lightning

storm, all things can change. For the better and for the worse. They say magic can happen and wishes can come true."

"Who is they?" I asked.

"You know," Joanie said. "They who know everything."

"Oh, *they*."

Joanie gave me a look. "What do you think of the new bride to be?" she asked, in an almost-whisper.

I nearly dropped the empty glass in my hand. Instead I dropped it into the dishwasher and looked at my friend. "What are you talking about? They're not getting married. I bet they haven't even slept together yet."

"Why not? Can Hayword still get it up?"

I rolled my eyes. "How would I know? I haven't had sex with him in years."

Joanie looked out the window over the sink. "He is still a good-looking man."

"Quit lusting after my husband," I said.

"Ex-husband," she said. No one knew we weren't divorced yet. It was no one's fucking business.

Joanie looked at me. "What's wrong with you? You've been nasty all day."

"Why did he invite us all here?" I asked. "To meet his fucking girlfriend? I don't want to meet his new fuck buddy."

"I thought you said—"

I put my hands up. "There's too much going on. Can't he keep it in his pants until we get this film finished?"

"Hey, you brought Mark around all the time, and Hayword never said anything."

"That's because Harwood is a fucking saint," I said. "And I am not."

"Brooke."

"I took a drink," I said. "I wasn't thinking, and I took a gulp of wine."

Joanie put her glass down and put her arms around me. "Oh, baby," she said.

I wondered if this was what it was like to be caught in the Iron Maiden.

"Get off me," I said, a little harsher than I meant.

Joanie let me go.

"Do you want to go to a meeting?" Joanie asked.

I was sorry I had told her, but then she had helped me dress a naked dead man, and I had pulled her toe out of a bathtub faucet, so we didn't have many secrets between us.

"No," I said. "I took the one sip." Ahhh, now it had gone from a gulp to a sip. "I want to forget about it. It'll be OK."

"It's Mark, isn't it?" she said. "He was so good for you. Have you broken up again? Now that the restaurant is closed it must be weird living there."

I sighed. "It was never right after the earthquake," I said. "I was in the bungalow more than I was at our place." I shrugged. "We are so different. It was bound to happen."

"Wait," Joanie said. "Does Mark know you are broken up?"

I snorted.

"Come on," she said. "You don't like goodbyes or endings or any of that. I could see you sneaking out and—"

"Shut up," I said. I ignored her question. Because I didn't know if Mark knew. Once the restaurant closed, he went back to being a plumber, and his clients were closer to his old home. So he often stayed at his old house. I often stayed at the bungalow. We texted. But we hadn't actually spoken in days.

"Hollywood sucks the life out of you," I said.

Joanie laughed. "Give me a break. You are enjoying the fame and the game."

"No, I am not. For one thing, I don't have the fame. And I've never been game."

Truth was life had been more fun when I was drunk. Hadn't it? I squinted. That couldn't be true.

"Where's Marv anyway?" I asked. "Are you still married? I haven't seen him in ages. Maybe years. Did you kill him and bury him in your backyard?"

Joanie laughed. A screechy nervous laugh. She picked up her glass and emptied it into her mouth. And swallowed.

"If this was a horror movie," I said, "you would now be a suspect in a murder plot."

"I didn't murder him," Joanie said. "But I haven't heard from him for a while. I think he might want a divorce. We had a big fight before he want on a trip. He left three weeks ago, and I haven't heard from him. You know he goes to visit his brother in Mali every few years. He doesn't communicate much when he's there. I think he and Marty go out and pick up women."

"In Mali?" I asked. "That's a long way to go to commit adultery."

"Adultery?" she said. "No, he just has a few fucks. He's careful. I'm sure."

"About as careful as you are," I said.

"Hey!" she said.

I shrugged. "Truth to power, sistah. Well, truth to slut. From slut."

Joanie laughed. "Anyway, I finally called his phone, and he doesn't answer. I left a message with his brother and didn't hear back. Finally got his brother's house, and they said he was out on safari, or whatever they call it. I asked about Marv, but the houseboy, or whatever he was, didn't seem to know what I was talking about. So I'm a little concerned."

I stared at her. "A little concerned? Jesus. Your husband has been missing for three weeks!"

"Hey, you know we live very separate lives," she said. "We

like it like that. I was giving him space, and I thought he was giving me space."

"Did you check his credit cards," I asked, "to see if he was using them and where?"

"Check his credit cards?" she asked. "How would I do that?"

"Jesus, woman. Aren't they your credit cards, too? You'd look it up online."

"You are harshing my mellow. He's been gone for this long before. I'm sure he's fine."

"How are you going to explain it to the police if he's not?" I asked.

"What do you mean?" She suddenly looked alarmed.

"If someone has hurt him and you never filed a missing person report, won't they suspect you of foul play?"

"You've been watching too many crime shows, Mac," she said. "Let's forget about it. Are you staying at the bungalow tonight? Come up to the house tomorrow, and we can go through Marv's papers. You're better at this sort of thing. I bet you'll figure it out."

"Better at what sort of thing?" I asked.

"Sneakiness," she said.

She left the kitchen. I felt a tinge of dizziness, like the beginning of an altered state of consciousness. I glanced around the kitchen. Were all the glasses emptied? Yes. Fuck. But that bottle of wine didn't look quite empty. I hurried across the room, picked up the dark bottle, put it up to my lips and opened my throat. Liquid red gold flowed into my body. I gulped and gulped.

When I stopped, I let out a long sigh, wiped my mouth, and poured the rest of the wine down the drain.

"Hey, that's good wine," Hayword said, as he came into the kitchen. "I would have put a cork in it so I could have it tomorrow."

"Too late," I said. "It's all gone."

The monster was now coursing through my whole body. I felt free and devastated all at the same time.

I leaned against the counter again and smiled at Hayword.

"Soooo," I said. "Must be love."

He looked at me, frowned a bit, and then shrugged. "You mean Patricia? She's fun."

"Unlike me," I said.

Hayword went to the sink and began putting dishes in the dishwasher, taking over my unfinished job.

"What's going on, Brooke?" he asked. "You don't like Patricia?"

I shrugged. I had my hand up, as if it now contained a glass of wine. What *was* going on? I wanted to scream, "Please, help me, Hayword. It's happening all over again." But I didn't.

"No one is funnier or more fun than you," Hayword said.

Joanie was right. Hayword was still good-looking. That had never been the problem. The problem was that he had always been insecure, was always looking for adulation or—approval. At least that was what he was like when we were married. Now that he was a successful producer, he wasn't quite so needy. Maybe he would be better in bed now. Not that he had ever been bad.

I walked up to him and put my hand on his back. We shocked each other and both jumped. He turned partway around and looked at me. "What was that?"

"I dunno. I guess we have electricity." I smiled. I felt more dizzy. I blinked hard. It was almost as if someone else had control over my body.

Almost.

Hayword laughed. "Like the kind of electricity in an electric chair, the kind that kills? I would agree with that."

"Hey, we weren't bad together," I said. "Don't rewrite history. Except for the part when you fucked some blonde bimbo after our son died."

"And you fucked every hair color under the sun," he said. "We're lucky we don't have an SDS."

"An SDS? Wasn't that a terrorist group in the sixties?"

He frowned and looked up as he tried to remember. "Oh yeah. STD."

I laughed, and he grinned.

"I'm feeling a little dizzy," I said. "Do you think you could drive me home?"

Hayword glanced outside.

"You'd be in and out before anyone knew you were gone," I said.

He looked at me, his expression saying the same thing I was thinking. What was I doing?

"Please," I said. "I don't want to worry about going around those curves and ending up careening off the mountain."

"Let me go tell Patricia I'm leaving," he said.

"No need," I said. "You'll be right back. I promise."

He hesitated, and then he nodded. We went out the front door together and got into Hayword's little sports car. I thought it was ridiculous for a man his age—or any age—to be tooling around in something like this. I didn't know the model. I didn't care. I drove a sedan. Just like any sensible person would.

I texted David. "Dad's taking me home. Don't worry if he doesn't get back right away."

Crap. I was feeling cranky again.

I needed another drink.

Hayword drove quickly down our canyon road—but not too quickly. He didn't look at me, but he kept asking me questions.

"How is Mark doing?"

"Fine." I wasn't gonna tell him nuthin'.

"I haven't seen Fern lately," he said. "She doing well?"

"You don't know? She is your daughter."

"She's your daughter, too," he said. "So how is she?"

"How would I know?" I said. "She did stop by my house on Friday when I wasn't there. Left me a little present. I think she's trying to be nice. You should see her sometimes. You're at the studio more than I am."

"Yeah, how is the script coming along?"

"Just fine." My buzz was starting to wear off. Maybe that was a good thing. Maybe that would stop what was about to happen.

We were almost at my bungalow.

"You love this Patty woman?" I asked.

"Patricia. And no."

He drove up my drive and stopped the car. He didn't turn off the engine.

"You're not gonna walk a girl to the door?" I asked.

"You're not a girl," he said, "and usually you don't want me anywhere near this place."

"Well, I fucked a lot of people here," I said. "I didn't want you to have any bad memories."

We got out of the car, walked up the steps together, and went into the bungalow together. It smelled like cinnamon inside.

"Why would I have bad memories?" Hayword said. "You never fucked me here."

"We can change that tonight," I said as I walked back to the bedroom. I switched on the light and began stripping off my clothes.

"Um, wait, what? Mac, why are you taking off your clothes? Stop it."

I smiled. "Come on," I said. "For old times' sake. You can go back to Patricia, and she'll never know."

"I'll know," he said.

"Have you fucked her yet?"

"That's none of your business."

I pulled my pants off—and now I was standing in front of Hayword naked.

I walked to him and put my arms around his neck. He didn't move. He looked down at me.

"What's going on?" he asked gently.

I leaned against him. I could feel his erection.

"What about Mark?" he asked.

"What about Mark?" I said. "It's only us here, Hayword. Like it used to be when we were kids writing *Love and Other Insanities.*"

"Is this love or insanity?" he asked.

"Does it matter?"

He put his arms around me, and we kissed. It felt so familiar. A few moments later, he was naked. We were on the bed together. As soon as his penis was inside me, I felt the same way I had when I took the drink: wonderful and devastated all at the same time. What was I doing? What was I thinking? How on Earth had this all happened?

"It's always only been you, Brooke," Hayword said as we moved together.

Oh fuck.

What had I done?

CHAPTER TWO

Strangely I dreamed of Katherine and Oscar, the couple who had produced and financed our first movie *Love and Other Insanities* all those years ago. In the dream, they kept telling me everything was going to be OK.

I woke up to a pulsing headache. I sat up slowly. The room tilted a bit. I put my head in my hands. Was I such a fucking amateur that I had a hangover from the equivalent of a glass or five of wine?

"Fuck, fuck, fuck," I murmured.

I heard a stirring in the bed.

Then I remembered what had happened. Shit. Everything was not going to be OK. What I had done? Jesus H.

I got up, grabbed my clothes, and hurried out of the room. I closed the door softly—I hoped. My head was throbbing too loudly for me to know for certain. I switched on the light in the living room, got quickly dressed, and then sat on the sofa. It was 9:30 p.m. It was still the same day I had taken a drink.

I looked around the room. I felt terrified.

I breathed deeply. Once. In and out. Twice. In and out. Looked around.

So much had happened in this house over the years.

The lovers I had brought here while on a drunk I had pretty much forgotten. But this was where I had written the first two *Beauty and the Zombie* scripts. This was where Fern had told me she thought she had burned down our house. This was where I found a movie executive dead—and dressed only in fishnet stockings. This bungalow had survived an earthquake and a wildfire. It had survived me being a drunk for many years. It had survived me being sober for many years.

But it had never felt like home.

I rubbed my eyes. I tried to remember the last time I felt at home anywhere.

I couldn't.

No place felt like home.

Ugh.

Why had I taken that first drink? Why on Earth had I slept with Hayword? We had survived the fire at our first house. We had survived the wildfire and earthquake here. We had finally come to terms with the death of our son, Alberto. We had come through my alcoholism. Well, Hayword and I were almost divorced, so we hadn't come through it as a couple. But we survived. We were friends.

Hayword and I not being divorced was a constant source of tension between Mark and me. He didn't understand why Hayword and I were still married. I didn't understand why it mattered. It wasn't as if Mark and I were going to get married. You got married if you were gonna have babies. Otherwise, why bother?

Christ.

I had taken a drink. I had slept with Hayword.

What now?

I was supposed to be working. My script for *Beauty and the Zombie: Whackadoodle Times* was overdue. Sally St. James kept bugging me about it. It was our studio now: Sally, Hayword, and I owned it. Sally and Hayword ran it. I was the talent, so to speak. Back to Life Studios we called it. *Beauty and the Zombie Three* would make or break us.

I had worked under a deadline before. I had done it drunk; I had done it sober. I could do it now.

Yet for some reason I had barely written a word of it.

That could not be why I picked up that drink.

It could not be why I slept with Hayword. Could it?

Fuck. Why was I asking myself these stupid questions? Again. I was going in circles. I drank because I was a fucking addict.

I grabbed my purse and keys and stepped outside onto the porch. Then I realized I had left my car at Hayword's house.

Fuck, fuck, fuck.

I went back into the house, set down my purse, and tiptoed into the bedroom. I closed the door enough to shut out the light. Then I went to the chair where Hayword had thrown his trousers. I reached into the front pocket and felt around until I found his keys. As I pulled them out, the keys jangled, and Hayword made a noise. I stayed very still and listened to the darkness until I heard him sleep-breathing. Then I left the room and the house again, closing the doors quietly behind me.

I took Hayword's car down to the village. I felt stupid driving a little sports car. It seemed dangerous. I didn't feel drunk any longer, but what if I was? What if I got stopped and got a DUI? It would be all over the papers.

I parked in front of one of the small markets in the village that sold liquor. An all-nighter. It was only 9:30 p.m.—not 2 a.m.—but the lights in the store were still too bright for me. I put on my sunglasses and went to the cooler first and got a jug of orange juice. Then I went straight to the vodka. Still remembered where it was. I plopped them both down on the countertop. A pale woman rung them up without touching them. Unless she did it very quickly. I gave her the money she asked for.

"Early breakfast," she said. "I remember those days."

I looked at her through my sunglasses.

"Yes," I said. "I'm an alcoholic, and this is what I have for breakfast, lunch, and dinner. Well, it's what I used to have. Haven't had a drink in five years until tonight. Tonight I decided to celebrate."

"Celebrate what?" the woman asked as she slipped the vodka in a bag and then put that bag into another one with the orange juice.

"The fact that the world is just too fucking scary," I said.

The woman laughed.

I took the bag from her and asked, "What's so funny?"

"How can the world be scary to you?" she said. "You have everything."

"You don't know anything about me," I said.

She nodded. "Yes, I do."

I squinted. Did I know her? She looked vaguely familiar.

"You're an alkie, too," I said.

She looked at me. I nodded. "Don't mind me. I'm not a good alcoholic or a good sober."

"I'll go to a meeting with you."

"What? You're standing behind that counter selling poison to people, and you're offering to go to a fucking meeting with me? How hypocritical are you?"

"It's not poison to everyone," she said with very little expression. I suddenly felt like I was in one of my movies. Was she a zombie, too?

"Be careful of the paps," she said. "They like to follow

celebrities after they've bought liquor. I've seen it happen several times."

"Paps are such assholes," I said. "But I'm not a celebrity. No one is gonna follow me. Thanks. Stay sober."

I hurried out to the car. What I used to do was drain out half the orange juice and then pour the vodka into the jug. Instant screwdriver. In case any paparazzi were hanging around, I decided to wait. I drove carefully up the winding road back to my house.

I went inside quietly, listened for any movement, didn't hear any, so I tiptoed into the kitchen. I got a glass and filled it 2/3rds with orange juice. Without hesitation, I took the seal and cap off of the vodka. I unscrewed it, and I poured it into the glass until the glass was full. I opened the pantry door, moved some boxes around, and hid the vodka behind them all. I put the vodka-spiked OJ in the fridge, next to the almost empty bottle of Martinelli's Fern had left me. Then I stood over the sink, and I drank the vodka-laced orange juice, slowly, until I emptied the glass. I rinsed it out and stood at the sink.

It was as if a decision had been made a long time ago that I was going to drink again, and tonight was the night. I didn't get it. I didn't understand it. But I didn't fight it. It was a relief not to fight it.

I felt like I was going to throw up.

Liquor on an empty stomach. Gawd.

I scrambled a couple of eggs. Then I sat on the couch and ate them while I became drunk again. I felt sick and dizzy, but I didn't feel anxious. I didn't feel stressed. I didn't feel much of anything.

I heard my name from far away. I opened my eyes to daylight. I blinked. My head throbbed again. My eyes finally focused. Hayword was leaning over me. I had fallen asleep on the couch.

"It's OK," Hayword was saying. "It's just me."

"What? Yes." I sat up.

"You looked so scared just now," he said. "Why didn't you wake me?"

"What? Oh, I was a little hungry," I said. "I must have fallen asleep after I ate."

He sat on the couch next to me and put his hand on my arm. I wanted to slap it away.

"What happened yesterday?" he asked.

"Um, weren't you there?" I said. "We had sex."

"It feels like—it feels like you seduced me," he said.

I did slap his hand, and he pulled it away.

"What the fuck are you talking about?" I asked. "I didn't seduce you."

"I think you wanted to have sex with me for some reason," he said. "And it happened."

"You didn't want to have sex with me?" I asked.

I got up and moved to the chair. I pulled my feet up underneath me.

"Of course, I did," Hayword said. "I love you. That has never gone away. But I didn't think you felt the same way."

"I honestly don't know what happened," I said. I knew I should tell him that I had started drinking again. I knew I should go to a meeting right then and there. If I wanted to get sober again, I had to be honest.

But I didn't know if I wanted to be sober again. It was a lot of fucking work.

"I was jealous of Patricia," I said. "I guess."

He nodded. "I'll have to tell her this happened."

"Why? Are you two exclusive?"

He shook his head. "We haven't even slept together yet."

"I knew it," I said.

"What?"

"Nothing."

"And Mark," Hayword said. "We'll have to tell Mark. I wouldn't want to betray him."

"Betray him?" I said. "I don't belong to him or to you. I can fuck whomever I like."

"That's all it was?" he asked. "A fuck? You wanted to keep me on the hook for yourself like some little lap dog."

"You are mixing metaphors," I said. "Or whatever. I'm sorry. I don't know what's going on."

He looked away from me and shook his head. "We just left the house. We didn't tell anyone. They must have been worried sick."

"I texted David last night."

"That's something." He looked at me again. "I don't know what's going on with you, but I hope you're OK. I hope I didn't screw anything up for you. I had waited a long time for you to want me again, and that was . . . irresistible."

Oh crap. What a piece of scum I was. He was having all of these feelings, and I was having none. I knew what to do. I leaned toward him and held out my hand. He took it, and I squeezed his.

"You've always been a hunk in my eyes," I said.

Hayword chuckled. "OK. Knock it off. I'll take you back to the house and you can get your car. I can make you breakfast after I take David to school. Remember his car is in the shop."

I had forgotten how charming he could be.

"I do need my car," I said, "but I've got that script to work on, so I better come right back here. Hey, I dreamed about Katherine and Oscar just now. Isn't that strange? I always liked them. They liked us. Thought we would go all the way together."

Hayword nodded. "They have their OK Studios out in the country now."

Ah, that's why they kept telling me everything was OK.

"It's a really nice place," Hayword said. "I think you'd like it."

"You've been?" I asked.

He nodded. "I've kept in touch over the years. They tried to keep in touch with you, but you were never interested."

I nodded. I had no memory of that. Another one of my failings, I supposed.

I wasn't in the mood.

"I should probably give them a call," I said. I smiled. I would never call them. What would I say? "Hey, you haven't heard from me in 15 years, but here I am now."

A few minutes later, Hayword drove us back to the house. David came out before Hayword stopped the car. He cocked his head slightly as he looked at us.

Fuck.

We got out of the car.

"Hi, darlin'," I said. "It's nice to see you, but I gotta get going."

David held up his hands and blocked the way to my car and to the house.

"Where were you?" he asked.

"Your mom wasn't feeling well," Hayword answered.

"And you couldn't text or call Patricia?" David asked. "That was so rude, Dad."

Hayword looked at me. I shrugged. "It was a family matter," I said. "She'll get over it."

David said, "You say that like she doesn't matter."

I bit my tongue so that I didn't say what I wanted to say: She didn't matter.

"She's a human being," David said.

"What are you so mad about?" I asked. "You met her all of once."

"It's a crappy thing to do," David said. "Like something you would do when you were drinking."

I could feel Hayword's eyes on me. I looked up at David.

"I am sorry," I said. "It was rude. I'll call her and apologize."

"Are you drinking, Mom?" David asked. He occasionally asked me this when I was doing something he didn't like.

"Of course not," I said. "I can stay if you like. Dad offered to make breakfast."

"I already ate," David said. "Dad, we need to hurry or I'll be late for school. And you haven't done anything to the house for the lightning storm. They said we should put up storm shutters and make sure everything is grounded."

"It's just a storm," Hayword said. "Everything is grounded. We have storm shutters. We have a generator."

"We could all be fried," David said. "In the Luxembourg storm, 300 people died."

"That was 200 years ago," Hayword said. "And munitions blew up. We don't have any munitions."

"You don't know," David said. "For all we know one of our neighbors is a rightwing white supremacist with a barn full of explosives."

"Then they'll die in a fiery blast, and we will be fine," Hayword said. "Besides, the guy predicting this could be all wrong. Normally they can't predict electrical storms."

"The *guy* has been studying climate change for decades, and he found some unexpected atmospheric parameters that allowed him to develop a prediction model for lightning storms," David said. "When he applies the algorithm to current conditions, he can predict lightning storms with 94% accuracy within 4-5 days. I looked it over. It seems solid."

Of course David had looked over the evidence. Good for him. I had not realized how worried he was about this.

"It's going to be OK," I said.

"You don't know anything!" he said. He turned and went into the house. He sounded like Fern.

"When is this storm supposedly coming?" I asked Hayword.

"Wednesday or Thursday," he said. "Is David right? Are you drinking? Did you just stand here and lie to our son?"

"I did not," I said. "I am not drinking."

He nodded. "Ahhh, the literal defense. Fuck." He leaned his head back. "You were drinking. I should have known. Well, I'm not doing this again, Brooke. I can't. I won't. I can't believe you made me a part of your sickness."

I laughed. "You were always a part of my sickness, Hayword. You know that. The death of our son. You fucking someone else."

"I'm not falling for that," he said. "You had a hole in your soul as wide as the Grand Canyon before any of that happened. If you remember, he wasn't my son. You had fucked someone else and gotten pregnant."

"How dare you say he wasn't your son!" I said a little too dramatically. "I knew it. You never loved him."

Hayword made a noise. "This is old stuff, Brooke. We've been over it. We've healed it. It's finished. Don't start it again. Your outrage is about as fake as . . . as you are."

My stomach knotted. For a moment, I felt like myself again: full of guilt and doubt.

"I know," I said. "I know. I don't know what's wrong with me. I don't know what happened."

Truth peeked out again.

"Please," I said, "don't leave me."

Oh fuck. What was that? I sounded so pathetic.

"You left me a long time ago," Hayword said. He shook his

head. "I'll take you to a meeting, but beyond that, you are on your own."

"Really? I make one slip in five years and suddenly I'm evil and worthless, and you're gonna cut me loose?"

"You got drunk and you fucked me," he said. "It wasn't because you loved me or wanted me. You wanted to take me away from Patricia, as though I were your plaything that had gotten away. You wanted to show me that you could have me if you wanted. That's cruel, Brooke. That's fucking cruel. The woman I loved would never have done anything like that. Ever."

I stared at him. Then I sighed. I was as perplexed as he was.

"The woman you loved died a long time ago," I said. "Ain't that the truth? We've been waiting for her to come back all these years that I've been sober, haven't we? But I just kept going from one emergency to another. Getting through one thing only to go through another. And now that things are almost normal, I realize . . . I am not."

"Sounds like a crock of shit to me," Hayword said.

Wow. He was angry.

"Are you going to a meeting or not?" he asked.

I laughed. "You just said you didn't want anything to do with me. So whether I go to a meeting or not is none of your fucking business."

"Don't forget David's car is in the shop," Hayword said. "You need to pick him up after school. He's got a club until 4:00."

I got into my car and drove away. I didn't want to look back, but I did. Hayword was not staring after me. He had walked into the house and closed the door. I could almost feel him slamming it.

I began to cry. Or rather I tried to make myself cry. Didn't work.

What had happened?

It didn't matter, didn't matter.

I needed to go to a meeting. And listen to the pathetic stories of all the people who were as pathetic as I was? I shook my head as I continued up the road a bit and then drove into Joanie's driveway. She ran out her front door toward my car. I slammed on the brakes. As usual, she was barely dressed, wearing something beige and mostly sheer with red high heels. I turned off the car.

"Mac!" she yelled as I got out. "You were right. I looked at the credit card statements."

She looked terrified. I sighed. OK. We would deal with her fake drama first.

"And?"

She grabbed my hand. "Marv hasn't used them. Mac, he must be dead!"

CHAPTER THREE

"Did he take out any cash before he left?" I asked.

"Just a thousand dollars," Joanie said. "Pocket money, you know."

"OK."

"Where is he?" she asked. "What's happened?"

"How would I know? Maybe you should call the police."

"But you said they're going to ask why I didn't call before."

We walked into the house. Her housekeeper Maria was nowhere in sight. We sat in the living room. A plate of scrambled eggs and a martini glass rested on the glass coffee table. Huge picture windows looked out at the back of her property. She picked up the martini glass and emptied the contents into her mouth.

"Oh," she said. "I'm sorry. Should I hide the martini glass or get you a drink?"

I blinked. Really? She would get me a drink? I didn't know if that was awful or generous.

"No," I said. "I'm good. So when did you last see Marv? Did you check if he took his scheduled flight?"

She shook her head. "I have no idea how I would actually do that. That morning he came into the bedroom and kissed me goodbye."

"Did he say anything?"

"He said he'd see me in a month," she said. She closed her eyes. "And then we fucked. Oh no. Wait. That wasn't him. No, Ronnie came that morning. Literally and literally. It was her day."

"Her day?" I had met Ronnie. Back when I was drinking and fucking everyone, I had fucked her, too. She was young and bored. And pretty good in bed. I hadn't known she and Joanie were a thing.

"Um, I thought you leaned toward the tall dark and penis laden," I said. "Ronnie?"

Joanie shook her head. "Something about her. She's got a tongue that will not quit."

I didn't like the idea that Joanie and I had had sex with the same person. It felt incestuous. Or something. Icky.

"Anyway, Marv kissed you goodbye."

"Said he was taking the Jag to drop it off at the dealer's," she said. "I had forgotten that."

"I assume the Jag is gone," I said.

"I assume so," she said. "It's in the other garage at the bottom of the property, where we used to keep the horses. He has a few of his more expensive cars there."

We looked at each other.

I said, "People go down to that garage regularly, though, right? Your landscapers or workmen or you?"

Joanie shook her head. "No. It's Marv's garage. No one goes down there. I've been there probably twice in twenty years."

Oh fuck, fuck, fuck.

"We better call the police," I said.

"No," Joanie pleaded. "Not yet. Let's at least go to the garage. See if he took the Jag like he said."

"Joanie, he could be there. Dead."

"No," she said. "Maybe he got into an accident on the way to the airport, and he's lost his memory."

"And his ID?"

"Please," Joanie said.

"Get some shoes on at least," I said.

"These are shoes," she said.

I rolled my eyes. She ran upstairs. A few minutes later she came down dressed in slacks and a shirt and wearing flats. She looked unlike herself.

"Wait," I said. "Don't you have security cameras all over the place? We can look at those."

"No," Joanie said. "We keep them up, but they don't work. They were always a pain in the ass."

We went out the back door and walked down the long mani-cured lawn.

"This looks too perfect," I said. "Do you use chemicals on it? David would be so disappointed."

"I don't know," she said. "Like I pay attention."

"David says that's what's wrong with the world. People don't pay attention."

"I love David, but he should enjoy himself more."

"Hey, leave him alone," I said. "He's perfect the way he is."

"He's an anxiety bomb waiting to go off," Joanie said. "Did you go to a meeting?"

"Not yet," I said.

We neared a low wooden building. Looked like a four car garage. Joanie peeked through the window on the side door.

"The Jaguar is in there," she said. She looked at me. She bit her lip.

"Open the fucking door," I said.

And so she did. We were hit with a wave of stink. Dead body stink. Shit, shit, shit. Joanie turned around and threw up. I covered my mouth and looked inside. I could definitely see a figure in the driver's seat of the Jaguar. I backed out of the garage and shut the door.

"Was it Marv?" Joanie asked.

"I don't know," I said, "but someone is dead in there. Did you bring your phone?"

She shook her head.

"Did he kill himself?" she asked. "Did someone kill him? Did he have a heart attack and die there?"

"I don't know," I said. "We need to call the police."

She nodded and started to cry.

"I'm sorry, Joanie."

"He was a good man," she said.

I didn't say anything. I didn't know if he was a good man or a bad man. I took her hand, and we walked back up toward the house. I did not want to stay for the coming shit storm. I needed to go to a meeting. Or go get a drink.

We went back into the house. I picked up her phone on the coffee table and held it out to her.

She said, "Wait. Let's think about this. I don't know if he left a will."

"You don't know if he left a will?" I repeated. I was astonished.

"What if he didn't leave me anything?" she said. "His kids could take it all. I need time to move some cash around before I call the police."

"Joanie!" I said. "You have to call the police now."

"You didn't call the police when your guy died in fishnet stockings," she said. "I helped you dress him before you called the police."

"OK, yes. But he wasn't my guy. If you move money around the day you call the police, they'll know something is up."

"Well, we can wait a few days. I'll tell the police I was worried he had left me, so I wanted to make sure I got my share, in case they ever ask. They won't ask. Marv has money in places that no one knows about, except me. Unless he mentions it in a will. I need some time."

"You're comfortable leaving a dead man in the garage?" I asked.

"Have some respect," Joanie said. "That dead man is my husband. And yes, he's been there for three weeks. Another couple days won't hurt anything."

"Oh my gawd. I feel like I'm in a Faulkner story. Or one of my movies."

"He's not coming back from the dead," Joanie said. "I want to get my fair share before his greedy children take it all."

"We need to call the police," I said.

"And you need to go to a fucking meeting," Joanie said. "But you aren't going and I'm not calling the police."

We stared at each other.

"Jesus, Brooke," she said. "Why don't you have a drink? You were so much more fun when you were a drunk."

I raised my eyebrows. Gotta admit: That stung. It was what I always feared.

"It's true," she said. She picked up the martini mixer on the coffee table and poured the liquid into her glass. She wiped her lipstick off the edge, and then she held the glass out to me.

"We have to walk on glass around you all the time," she said. "So that we don't upset you so much that you drink or fuck or whatever. It's exhausting. And you're always so sure of everything, that you're right, that AA saved you. It's pompous. It is fucking boring."

I took the glass from her and emptied the contents into my

mouth and swallowed. Martinis were never my drink, but what the hell.

"I think you meant you all walk on eggshells around me," I said.

"What?"

"You walk on eggshells, not on glass," I said.

She shook her head. "Whatever. Just don't tell anyone. Let me take care of this myself."

I laughed. "When have you ever been able to take care of things yourself?"

"Look around," she said. "I've got everything I ever wanted. I did that."

"You married this," I said. "What did you ever do to earn it?"

"I fucked him," she said. "That's what I did."

"Your grief is touching," I said.

We were supposed to be best of friends. What had happened?

"Mac," she said, her voice suddenly soft and friendly again. "I'm in shock. I don't mean anything. Please, don't call the police. Let me get things in order, and then I'll call the police. I promise."

"Hey, it's not my funeral," I said. I tossed the martini glass toward the fireplace. It shattered on the stone floor. "Oops. I'm so clumsy. Now see: That's glass. Try walking on that instead of eggshells."

I hurried out of the house and got into my car.

"What the fuck," I said out loud as I drove quickly away. I always knew Joanie was a little different, but this was downright dangerous. She could go to jail. Now that I knew about it, could I go to jail, too? For what? Not disclosing a dead body? I would tell them I was doing research on my next script. No, no. If this blew up, got in the media, it could ruin the studio. Who would want to work for such a sleazy outfit? I laughed. That hardly made a difference these days, did it?

It was just after 8:30. I had time to get to a 9 a.m. meeting, one I rarely attended. Wouldn't see anyone I knew. Didn't want to tell anyone I was drinking. Didn't want to tell anyone *else*. Not yet.

So I drove to the bungalow and got my screwdriver breakfast from the fridge and put it between my legs as I drove out of the canyon and into another one. Parked in the church parking lot. Saw a lot of pickups. I gulped some of the vodka orange juice. I already felt high from the martini. I guessed my tolerance for alcohol was low these days. That was good. I didn't need as much.

I groaned. I did not want to do this. I needed something else. Hayword wasn't gonna fuck me now. Maybe Sally would be up for it. No. She was married, had kids, and we worked together. *Come on, Brooke.*

Mark. We weren't officially over, right? I bet he'd take me back. He wouldn't care if I was drinking. He hadn't before. He minded it, but he liked fucking me better when I was drunk I bet. After all, he was a drunk, too. One who hadn't had a drink in how many years? I didn't know. We never talked about it. He went to his meetings. And I went to mine. When I went to mine.

"Brooke," I whispered. "Go to the meeting. Go to the meet-ing."

I watched the people filing through the open door to go downstairs to the meeting room. Suddenly I recognized one of the people heading toward the door. I hadn't seen him in a few years—not since I screamed at him in another parking lot after another AA meeting. I had been so pissed at him. Ryan Nichols: Alberto's baby daddy.

I pressed on the car horn. Everyone looked my way, even

Ryan. I opened the window so that my face was visible. Everyone else kept walking. Ryan stopped and stared at me.

I felt a lump in my throat. I had loved him so much at one point in my life. I had risked everything for him. Even my health: We hadn't used protection, and I had gotten pregnant. Then he left me. It was crazy what I had felt for him. Stupid. I couldn't imagine it now. Seemed like it happened to another person.

I waved him over. He hesitated and then started walking toward the car. As he got closer, I saw that he had aged very well in the intervening years. He was still gorgeous, and I remembered we had had a lot of fun making Alberto—even though we weren't trying to make a baby. We had done it up, down, turned around. He was very good at pleasure.

"Hello, Brooke," he said, stopping a few feet from the car.

"Hello, Ryan," I said. "You wanna blow this meeting and take a drive?"

"Um, why? So you can kill me?" he asked.

Last time I had seen him I had called him every name I could think of and then some. I hated him so much for leaving me and for not even knowing Alberto had been born.

But now . . . I didn't feel anything.

So I laughed. I hoped it was a charming laugh.

"No," I said. "I want to be spontaneous. Come on. You owe me for deserting me when I was pregnant."

He flinched.

"I swear," I said. "I have no weapons."

Ryan got into the car. We looked at each other.

What the fuck was I doing?

Maybe I should kill him, make him pay for what he did to me. To us. I could put him in the garage next to Marv. I laughed. I wasn't a killer. I was a lover.

"What's so funny?" Ryan asked.

"You got in the car with me," I said. "You're done for now."

I tore out of the parking lot. For a second, I wished I had Hayword's sports car.

"Do you know this area?" I asked.

"Sure," he said.

"Take me some place beautiful then," I said. "Where we can see the world."

"OK," he said. And he told me where to go as we talked, interrupting every once in a while to tell me to turn here or there. It was a beautiful blue day, but I noticed none of it. I kept thinking about how close Ryan was to me. Thought about how many times we had been naked together. How he had ruined my marriage to Hayword. No, it had already been ruined. I was tired of being Hayword's cheerleader back then, his midwife, his mother. We had our life in Hollywood that seemed so . . . vacuous. Even more so after the success of our movie *Love and Other Insanities*.

I hadn't much liked life in the Midwest either, before Hollywood. I thought life in Michigan was provincial, claustrophobic.

Maybe I just couldn't be happy anywhere.

"How are the kids?" Ryan asked.

"You mean the ones who aren't dead?"

"Jesus, Brooke."

I laughed. "This is who I am," I said. "You must have always known that. A fucking bitch on wheels. Isn't that what they used to say?"

"I don't know who says that," Ryan said.

"I remember you said it more than once when you were fucking me," I said.

"It was a compliment," Ryan said.

I laughed. He chuckled.

"The kids are fine," I said. He didn't need to know. "How are you? Married with children now?"

"No," he said. "Just trying to stay sober and live day by day. I've gotten some work directing low budget movies."

"Good for you," I said.

"That sounds so patronizing," he said. "I know you own a studio now with Sally St. James and Hayword. You two still together?"

"We haven't been together since I got sober," I said. "But yes, we run the studio together. Sort of. It's a small studio."

"Your zombie movies are blockbusters," he said.

"They aren't zombie movies," I said. "They are more rightfully called the living dead."

"Aren't the main characters called zombie aliens?"

"Yes, but when you say it out loud it sounds stupid."

He laughed. "I liked the movies. Especially the last one. Made me cry. The shot of Aiden's arm coming out of the grave. Her dead son coming to life. Beautiful. I can't wait for the next one."

I groaned. I didn't want to talk about this. I wanted to fuck. I wanted to fuck Ryan and then leave him.

"Is Aiden going to be alive in the next one?" he asked.

"That's a secret," I said.

"Because you don't know?"

I glanced over at him. Maybe he wasn't as stupid as I thought he was.

"Because in real life, dead sons don't come back to life," I said. "My son didn't come back to life. So, no, I don't know what to do next."

Shit. I hadn't realized that was the crux of my problem. How was I going to bring a dead half-zombie alien/half human back to life again? Again.

"I would love to have that problem," Ryan said.

"Would you now?"

Suddenly the road turned and ended in a small parking lot,

and we were somehow up on a hill or ridge looking out at the Pacific ocean.

I gasped. Even my alcohol-addled brain registered the beauty.

"How'd you do that?" I said.

He shrugged. "I found it one day when I was drunk. Almost went over the edge. That was the day I decided to go to rehab." He nodded, smiling at the memory.

I leaned over and kissed him. I practically fell into him. He did not pull away. We crawled into the backseat and began making out. I felt a rush of adrenalin and pleasure. I liked his smell. I liked his taste. I put my hand between his legs and felt his balls but not his penis. He tried to slip his hands into my pants.

"No," I said. "I can finger myself. I want to fuck you."

He kept kissing me, we kept rubbing each other. I felt like I could come any second. But he stayed as soft as over-done noodles.

I straddled him.

"Let me do you," he said.

"No. I want your dick." He had never been particularly adept at any oral or digital sex, if I was remembering correctly.

"Brooke," he whispered. "I can't."

"Why? Did they cut it off? Are you sick? Are you impotent?"

He nodded.

"What are you saying yes to?"

"I haven't had an erection for years now," he said.

"Really?" He couldn't have told me that before we drove up the mountain and I got all hot and bothered?

"After I got sober," he said, "it never got really hard again. And after a while, I couldn't get it up."

"Did you try any medication?"

"Once or twice," he said. "It got hard, but that was about it. I didn't feel anything."

"Who cares if you felt anything?" I said. "You could still give someone a good ride."

I was starting to lose my buzz and my desire.

"Honestly, Brooke," he said. "It got really bad after that time I saw you at the AA meeting. I had just found out that Alberto had died, and then you went after me. I stopped dating pretty much. And then, you know, it wouldn't get hard."

I laughed. "Are you blaming me for this? That's giving me a lot of power. Maybe you brought me up here to kill me?"

"Um, can we not talk about killing while my hands are in your pants?"

"Don't you want me," I asked as I kissed his ear. "You always wanted me."

Until I got knocked up.

I bit his ear.

"Ouch," he said.

I moved away from him and reached for my OJ jug. I took a swig. Then I held it out to him. "You want some?"

"What is it?"

"Orange juice," I said. He started to take it from me, but I pulled it back. Then I said, "It's got vodka in it."

We stared at each other.

"I'm sorry I left you," he said. "I'm so sorry about Alberto. I wish I had known him."

"He was a good boy," I said.

A tear rolled down his cheek. Or was it my cheek?

Ryan took the jug from me. His hands were shaking as he brought it up to his lips. And then he took several gulps and handed the jug back to me. I put it on the front seat again.

Then we began kissing. I pulled off my pants. I couldn't believe I was doing this. It was like something out of a dream. I opened the glove compartment and dug around until I found a condom. Then I straddled Ryan and undid his pants, unzipped him. He was hard as a rock. We pressed against one another. I put the condom on him. I was still proficient at that. Then I put his penis between my legs and pushed myself down on it. It hurt both of us a bit. He began to cry, and I moved up and down on him until we both had an orgasm, almost at the same time.

I wondered for a moment if it had been like this when we made Alberto. No. Ryan had never cried back then. And he had liked fucking me from behind most of the time, sometimes with me on my hands and knees like I was a fucking dog. Or he was a fucking dog? Never understood that. Did men have some secret fetish about acting like dogs or animals? Or was it that they didn't want to see our faces, they wanted to fuck us for the holes in our bodies?

So now on this mountainside, I was fucking Ryan because of all the holes in his body. Right? The holes in his soul.

Or maybe I was trying to fill up the monstrous hole in my own soul.

Naw. I couldn't have a soul. I had just handed an alcoholic a drink. And then I had fucked him.

I didn't know what was worse: Him leaving me after he found out I was pregnant. Or this, this moment, as I got off of him.

"Good news is there won't be an Alberto two," I said as I pulled my pants back on.

"Oh, great. Good news." He wiped the tears from his face and then zipped up his pants.

"See," I said, "you're cured. Now you can go fuck to your heart's content."

He stared at me. He looked absolutely ruined.

"I guess you did bring me up here to kill me after all," he said.

I opened my mouth to deny it. To tell him he had just had a great fuck and a good time. But I couldn't quite bring myself to say anything.

"Come on," I said. "I'll take you back to the church."

We got in the front seats again, and we drove away.

CHAPTER FOUR

We hardly said a word to one another as I drove back to the church. Every once in a while, Ryan picked up the jug of orange juice vodka and took a gulp. He stared out the window, mostly. I had thought revenge would feel a lot better than this—if that was what this was.

I stopped the car at the back of the church. Ryan opened the door to the car, got out, and walked toward the building. He did not look back.

I sure knew how to win friends and influence people.

I parked in the lot for a bit and checked my phone. I had texts from Sally, Fern, and David—and four from Mark. Nothing from Hayword. That meant he was still pissed. Nothing from Joanie. Maybe she had come to her senses and called the police about Marv. Dead Marv.

I read Sally's messages first.

"The investors want to talk to you," she wrote. "Can you come by today?"

Oh fuck. I had forgotten about investors. I had agreed to be a part of Back to Life Studios so I didn't have to deal with this kind of thing.

I texted back. "No. I'm busy. Another time?"

The phone rang almost immediately.

Fuck.

"Hi, Sally," I said. "How's it hangin'?"

"I don't know," she said. "I haven't seen it for a while."

"Trouble in paradise?" I asked.

"I dunno," Sally said. "Jonathan has seemed distracted lately. Won't tell me why. But who cares about real life. Why can't you come in today?"

"I've got things to do," I said.

"Like what?" she asked. "Are you working on the script? Because that's the only thing you should be doing."

"You aren't the boss of me," I said mildly.

"If we don't get this movie out, we're dead," Sally said, "and we will not come back to life. These guys are willing to give us some money."

"Can't I just fuck one of them?" I asked.

Sally laughed. "I have fucked you, and it ain't worth millions of dollars. Besides, we're respectable now. We don't do those kinds of things."

"Did you ever do those kinds of things?"

"Never," Sally said. She did not sound sincere.

"Spill," I said. "I'm in the mood."

"No," Sally said. She sighed. "It's a fucked up town, and we've all done some fucked up stuff."

"Not me," I said. "I am pure as the driven snow. I miss snow. Do you ever miss snow?"

"I'm from California," Sally said. "I don't miss any fucking snow. Come in and tell these guys about the movie."

"I want it to be a surprise," I said.

"So far that's working," Sally said. "The cast doesn't even have a treatment. We're filming in a month. Didn't we go through this last time?"

"And it all worked out," I said.

"I'll see you at Rio's at noon," Sally said. "I made a reservation."

"I can't make it downtown by then," I said.

"Do your best," Sally said. "And bring some pages."

She hung up.

"Well, fuck you, Sally," I said to the phone. "Fuck you, fuck you, fuck you."

I read Fern's text. Something about the character Molly in the movie. She made so many typos that it was difficult to read. David texted to say hello. "It was a good day today," he wrote. "I'm hearing some good ideas to combat climate change from the other kids."

I texted back, "You don't need to save the world."

He wrote back immediately. "Someone has to. You and Dad certainly didn't."

No, we had not saved the world. When had David turned into a little brat like his sister Fern? Fern was always mad at me. Now David was the same. Alberto would have been a teen now if he had lived. I wondered if he would have hated me, too.

I texted Joanie. "How's it going?"

"All good," she said. "All good. Sorry about the martini. I didn't mean to able you."

"Enable me."

"What?" she texted.

"You said 'able you.'"

"What's the difference?"

I sighed.

"Two letters."

"You at a meeting?"

I answered, "Yes, I am at a meeting."

This was exhausting. Best to ignore her.

I texted Hayword. "Are you up for a nooner?"

Why was I saying such things? I must have lost my mind yesterday. Was it the full moon? Had there been an alien invasion like in *Beauty and the Zombie?*

Hayword responded: "Your nooner is with Sally and our investors."

"I've never liked a crowd during sex," I texted.

"Have you gone to a meeting?"

They had all apparently forgotten how this works: They couldn't nag me into getting sober.

"I'm in the church parking lot right now."

Hayword didn't say anything, and that was pretty much the end of our conversation.

By the time I got back to the bungalow, I felt completely sober. I took a quick shower and put on jeans and a nice shirt. How else does a famous scriptwriter dress? I didn't drink anything. I hadn't been drunk for any Back to Life business, and I wasn't going to start now.

I got in my car, got onto the highway, and drove toward LA. When I neared Mark's exit, I remembered he had texted me, too, and I hadn't read them. I didn't know why. When we closed the restaurant, we both agreed to go back to our old houses for a while and reassess. He missed his friends and his mom. Beach life was too quiet for him. Me, too, really. I had thought I wanted to get away from all the bullshit of Hollywood, and once I was at the beach, I twiddled my thumbs. I waited for the next big catastrophe. I had fun when we were making movies, Hayword, Sally, and I. Otherwise, I was kind of antsy.

And once Mark and I got used to each other and weren't fucking every minute—and I wasn't drinking—life seemed kind of dull.

That was shocking to me. I got the quiet life I wanted, and then I didn't want it.

I needed to check in with Mark, but not this minute. I was going to be late getting to lunch as it was.

A valet parked my car, and I hurried into Rio's. I saw Sally at her favorite table with two young guys. My heart sank. I wasn't going to be seducing either of them. As I walked toward the table, I remembered Sally had said they were two tech guys who had made a lot of money doing something or another. I didn't care. Just give me your money.

The boys rose when I got to the table. The shorter one with blond hair and very white skin pulled out my chair, and I sat in it. The taller one with black hair and browner skin smiled. Sally introduced us. Damon Friend was the blond; Paolo Allende was the black-haired one.

I said, "It's cold and flu season so I don't shake hands. But I'm glad to meet you. Damon Friend. What a great name. Did you make that up?"

He smiled. "No, my parents were hippies. They wanted to be everyone's friends, and they loved Damon Runyon and Damon Knight's work."

I nodded. "That's interesting. Two very different writers."

"Guys and dolls, and it's a cookbook," Paolo said.

Damon rolled his eyes. "He's not a reader. He's more of a visual guy."

"Yep. I'm the movie guy," Paolo said. "I loved all your movies."

"Are you related to the writer Isabel Allende or her uncle Salvador Allende?"

"I wish," Paolo said. "Wouldn't that make a great movie? Tech entrepreneur is related to the great writer Isabel and the president the CIA assassinated?"

"He hasn't read a word she has written," Damon said. "Just so you know."

I smiled. I could like these kids.

"I ordered you a BLT," Sally said. "They have the best BLTs in the world here. Turkey bacon. Organic beefsteak heirloom tomatoes. Lettuce to die for. And gluten-free bread. Brooke loves them. Don't you, Brooke?"

I frowned. Sally sounded anxious. I grinned. "Whatever you order me, I will enjoy. Even got me some sparkling water while you all drink champagne. How fun."

"Well, you are driving," Sally said, giving me a look.

"I'm happy to hear you're interested in investing in Back to Life Studios," I said. "How can I help? As Sally has mentioned, I'm sure, I'm pretty much the writer. I leave the schmoozing and boozing to Sally and Hayword."

"Hayword is going to try to stop by," Sally said.

I frowned. "Really?"

"*Love and Other Insanities* is one of my old time all time favorite movies," Paolo said.

"It's not that old," I said.

"It's over twenty years old," Sally said. "They were about two. It's old to them."

"Ten," Paolo said. "I was ten. We know Katherine and Oscar Bernstein, by the way. They speak so highly of you. They said without you and Hayword's *Love and Other Insanities*, they wouldn't be the success they are today or have the catalog they have."

Weird. Their names had come up twice in one day.

"How kind," I said.

"I would love to have their catalog," Sally said.

"I heard rumors they might be retiring," Damon said, "And looking for someone to run the studios. Have you been out to their place? It is amazing."

"I have," Sally said. "Many years ago. My kids loved it. I'll have to check that rumor out. Or not." She shrugged. "I already have my dream job." She sounded like she was trying to convince herself.

Paolo said, "And the *Beauty and the Zombie* movies are so intense and so real," as if the conversation had never moved away from him. "I root for Colleen and her son Aiden—and Thomas. They are great characters. We're glad to hear that the old cast is returning."

"We start shooting in a month," Sally said.

The waitress brought our food. I was starting to get a headache. It was a little too noisy in here, and these kids were a little too intense.

We ate quietly for a few minutes. Then Damon said, "I met your daughter Fern the last time I came to the studio. She seemed nice."

"Fern nice?" I said. "Are you sure it was her?"

Sally St. James shot me a look.

I said, "I'm kidding. She's a treasure."

"She knows the business," Damon said.

"It is a family business," Sally said.

"I asked Fern about the story for the third movie," Damon said, "but she said she didn't know anything about it. You keep it pretty close to the vest."

"That's right," I said. "Plus we don't want it to get out and ruin the surprise."

"Is Aiden alive in the third one?" Paolo asked. "He'd have to be, wouldn't he? That was his hand that came out of the grave. That must feel so sweet, so cathartic, to make him alive, especially after what happened to your son Alberto. I figure the whole series is an homage to him, right? Aiden equals Alberto. The names both start with 'a.' They both died."

I stopped chewing. Sally's eyes widened. It seemed as if the whole restaurant stopped and we were all frozen in time and space.

I looked at Paolo. He was still chewing, completely oblivious.

"This time of year must be particularly difficult," Paolo said. "With Alberto's birthday and all."

I stared at him. Alberto's birthday? What was he talking about? It wasn't February. Wait. It was February. I closed my eyes. Fuck. Yesterday was his birthday. What the flying fuck? I had forgotten his birthday. Again. We had all forgotten his birthday. I felt like I was going to throw up.

"Paolo," Damon said. "That's pretty personal stuff."

The world began to throb. Or was that my head?

"I do my research," Paolo said. "They should know that."

"Who the fuck are you?" I said. I looked at Sally. "Who the fuck are these punks? Are you sure they don't work for the tabloids?" I looked at Paolo again. "Who the fuck are you to even say my son's name?"

"I-I thought it was common knowledge," he said. "And it happened so long ago. I figured it had been talked about before, in relation to your movies."

I pushed my chair away from the table and stood. I wanted to punch Paolo.

Just then, Hayword showed up. He looked at me. He was still angry with me. But then he must have seen my face—truly—and he knew something was wrong.

"What's going on?" Hayword asked.

"They were talking about Alberto's death," I said, "ten seconds after meeting me. Like it was fucking nothing. Mentioned his birthday yesterday." Hayword and I reached for each other's hands and hung on tightly.

Damon was standing now. Paolo looked perplexed.

"He didn't mean anything," Damon said.

"This meeting is over," I said.

Hayword and I hurried away. I was shaking as I walked out into the bright blue day. Handed the valet my ticket. He brought the car. Hayword and I got inside, and I drove down the block and parked it. We sat in silence.

"We forgot his fucking birthday," I said. "Again. We did that a few years ago. How come now?" I put my head on the steering wheel. "I guess that explains some things."

Hayword stared out the window. After a minute or two, he said, "I didn't forget his birthday. That's why we had the picnic yesterday."

"What?" I looked at him. "But you never said anything. And Fern wasn't there. We usually have a cake or a ceremony or something, all of us."

"We haven't done anything for a while," Hayword said.

"You should have said something. I forgot."

"Because you were drinking," Hayword said.

"No," I said. "No!" I was drinking now, but I wasn't then. I wasn't yesterday. Until I was.

That must be why I started drinking. It wasn't because my brain was fucked. Or I was fucked. I was still mourning the death of my baby son. I nodded.

"I'm sorry about yesterday," I said. "I don't know what happened."

I didn't look at Hayword, but I could see he was shaking his head.

"Did you call Patricia?" I asked.

"It's none of your business," Hayword said.

My phone buzzed. I looked down. "Get your ass back in here." From Sally St. James.

"Sally," I said. "She wants me back inside. Do we really need these guys?"

Hayword shrugged. "We're a small company. We need the

cash. Of course, normally we would have a script and know how much the production will cost."

"I've given you the treatment," I said. "They're making the sets."

"To answer your question then: Yes, we need the money."

"Why aren't you outraged that he asked about our son?"

"Why are you?" Hayword asked.

"It was such a shock," I said. "From strangers. We don't talk about it."

"It was a shock that he knew Alberto's birthday and you didn't?" he asked.

"Wow," I said. "That's mean."

"Takes one to know one," he said.

"Get out," I said. "I'm not going back to that meeting. If we need the money, you and Sally can get it. It's your job, not mine."

"They want to schmooze with you," Hayword said. "They want to see pages."

"When does anyone show investors pages?" I asked.

"All the time," Hayword said.

"I'm not showing pages to anyone," I said, "until I'm ready."

"Because you don't have any or because you don't want anyone to see them?"

"Hayword," I said. "Can't you trust me on this?" I put my hand on his arm. "It's the middle of the day. We could go home and fool around."

Hayword pulled his arm away. "I guess this means you're still drinking," he said, "because you'd only want to fuck me if you were drunk." He opened the car door.

"Not true," I said.

"You used to say that I acted like a child," he said. "I always wanted to be comforted. I wanted someone to hold me up and tell me things are gonna be OK. You said as adults we had to do things we didn't necessarily want to do. But when do you do something that you don't want to do?"

"All the time. Every minute of the day."

"Bullshit," he said. "We all work around you and your eccentricities."

"My eccentricities?" I said. "You mean my alcoholism?"

"Everything has to be your way," he said. "Otherwise you're going to break. We're all walking around trying to make sure we don't do anything that would cause you to break."

What was he talking about? Had he and Joanie gotten together to bitch about me?

"We need the money and you don't want to talk to these investors because they said something that hurt your feelings. How old are you?"

He got out of the car, shut the door, and walked away.

I didn't understand why he was so mad. I spent my life trying to fix all of their messes. Not the other way around.

I texted Sally, "Hayword is coming. I am not."

She texted back. "Don't be a fucking baby."

"Talking about my dead son = deal breaker."

I turned the phone off and then started the car.

"Fuck." I growled, turned the car off, got out, and practically ran to the restaurant. Nobody calls me a baby and gets away with it. I shook my head. I better never put that line in a script.

When I got to the table, Hayword was just sitting down again. They all looked up at me.

"You, Paolo, or whatever the fuck your name is," I said. I was talking rather loudly. "Don't mention my son's name again. Learn some manners. I don't know you, you don't know me. What if I brought up the fact that you're impotent most of the time even though you're only in your thirties."

Paolo looked around the restaurant. Then he looked at me, "But that's not true. It only happened—"

I held up my hand. "Boundaries, son, boundaries. Unless I'm fucking someone, I really don't want to hear about their potency problems. And even then, I don't want to hear it. Now I appreciate that you both like our films. That's great. We like fans. In fact, I could write in minor roles for you both, like extras, if you invest, if you'd like that."

Both their faces brightened, as if they were 10 year olds about to eat a trough of ice cream. Or whatever it was that caused 10 year old faces to brighten.

"That would be great," Damon said.

"Only you," I said, looking at Paolo, "your character will be an asshole. You good with that?"

Paolo nodded. "Absolutely."

"Good," I said. "Now I've got pages to write. And no, you're not gonna see them. Maybe in a few days I'll send you a scene or two. Maybe. If you don't piss me off."

I glanced at Sally. She winked at me. I sighed. Sometimes I did really miss fucking her. I glanced over at Hayword, but he didn't look at me. He was the fucking baby, not me.

I turned and walked away. I needed a drink or a fuck. Or an AA meeting. I'd take whichever came first. So to speak.

CHAPTER FIVE

For some reason, the freeway was not busy. I drove my car north like a bat out of hell. I didn't care if a cop stopped me. I felt free. Empowered. I had had a drink and the world had not ended. I was still here. My family was still safe. I had probably even saved the investment deal for Back To Life Studios with those punk kids. Whatever their names were.

I wasn't drinking now, but if I wanted to drink, I could. It would not be the end of the world. What a glorious feeling. The sky was blue. No catastrophic lightning storm in the works. I could almost smell the ocean. *I had had a drink and the world hadn't ended.*

Granted, I had fucked my almost ex-husband and my ex-lover all within the space of about twelve hours. That was excessive even for me. I still wasn't sure why I had done it—or done them. It didn't matter. Nothing mattered but the sheer pleasure I felt right that second.

I was coming up to the exit to Mark's house, so I took it. I wanted to spread around this feeling. And Mark and I had not had sex for a while.

I grinned as I drove toward his neighborhood. He would be glad to see me. No doubt. Of course it was in the middle of the day. He would probably be out working.

I turned down his street. I could see his driveway. His truck was parked there. Good. I wasn't sure how or why we had grown apart. He had stuck with me through everything. I thought the restaurant was his dream, but I was wrong. He only did the restaurant because he thought I would rather be with a chef than a plumber. He didn't realize I didn't actually care one way or another. I didn't know what I wanted to be when I grew up, so I thought I would help him be who he wanted to be. Turns out, being a plumber, hanging out with his friends, spending time with his mother, and being with me was what he wanted.

I parked my car in his driveway, glanced in the mirror, and then opened the car door, got out, and went to the front door. I had a key, but I knocked anyway. Then I tried the door. It was unlocked. I opened it and called, "Mark, it's Mac."

No one answered. I stepped inside and closed the door behind me. I felt a twinge of anxiety. I really didn't want to walk in on Mark on top of someone or in on someone on top of him.

"Mark!" I called again.

I walked into the living room. Everything looked the same as the last time I had been there. When had that been? Months? I went down the hall toward his bedroom. I steeled myself for what I was about to see. Mark was in bed, but he was by himself. And the room stunk of booze. A mixture of booze, urine, and vomit.

"What the fuck?" I said.

I hurried to the bed. Mark was snoring. Thank god. He was alive. Mark had been sober all the years I had known him. I shook him.

"What?" he mumbled. I shook him again.

"Mark! Wake up!"

He opened his eyes and pushed himself up. He blinked hard. "What? What?"

Good gawd, he stunk. And he looked like hell. I backed away from him.

"Mac," he said. He sat on the edge of the bed. "Finally. I've been texting you. I called, too. Where have you been?"

"I thought we were taking a break from one another," I said.

"A break?" He looked at me. "I don't remember that. I thought you were living at the bungalow for a while until we figured out where we wanted to live. Together."

I frowned. "Really? That's not how I remember it. But that doesn't matter now. What happened?"

He groaned. "I drank. Something terrible happened, and I picked up a drink. I'm so so sorry." He put his head in his hands and began to cry.

What the fuck? I had never seen Mark like this. He was always so dignified. So in control. So competent.

I did not like seeing this.

"Do you have any alcohol in the house?" I asked. Just in case I needed a quick boost. "You know, so I can throw it out."

"I dunno," he said.

I was not in the mood for anyone else's drama. I was supposed to be in love with this man, but I just wanted to run away.

What was wrong with me?

"I need to talk to you," he said. "Why didn't you answer your texts?"

"Mark, it stinks in here," I said. "Why don't you splash your face, and I'll meet you out in the living room."

He nodded. "I won't be long."

"Are you still drunk?" I asked.

He breathed deeply, stared at the wall for a second, and then said, "A little."

I left the room and closed the door behind me. I went to the kitchen and looked around. A bottle of whiskey. Two shot glasses. Someone had been drinking with him. And beer cans. What on earth had happened to him? What had happened to us? We had been together, and then suddenly we weren't. We had always led pretty separate lives, but after the earthquake a couple years ago—and then the second movie coming out—we just didn't seem to connect as much. Or something.

I opened the whiskey bottle. The smell nauseated me. I quickly put the cap back on. I opened the cupboards and looked around until I found a chocolate bar. 70% dark cacao. I quickly unwrapped it and began to eat it. If I could have had an orgasm while eating it, it would have been the perfect end of a really weird day.

Mark walked into the kitchen as I finished the chocolate bar. He was dressed in a clean white t-shirt and blue jeans. His hair was combed away from his face. He was as handsome as ever. I was so tempted to ask if he wanted to get naked, but I stopped myself.

Mark went to the sink, took the cap off the whiskey, and poured it down the sink. He threw the bottle into the recycle box and turned on the water until we couldn't smell the whiskey any longer.

"Do you want to talk about it?" I asked.

Mark shook his head. "Now you want to talk?"

"Are you mad at me?" I asked.

"No," he said. "I'm mad at me."

I took out my phone, turned it on, and waited. I heard the ping of several text messages and a voice mail. I searched for Mark's texts.

From Mark: "Please call. Having a difficult time."

I glanced up at Mark and then looked down again. Second message. "Brooke, please call me. I left you a voice message."

Third message: "I want a drink."

Fourth message: "I need you. Where are you?"

"Fuck," I whispered. I listened to my voice messages. One from David wondering where I was yesterday. One from Sally St. James asking when the manuscript would be finished and telling me to call her ASAP, from today. One from Mark: "Have you dropped off the face of the earth? Where are you? I need you." Two days ago.

"I'm sorry, Mark," I said. "I didn't see any of these."

"Why were you ignoring me?" he asked.

"I wasn't," I said. "It was Alberto's birthday yesterday. I guess I've been kind of depressed. I was ignoring everyone." That wasn't true, but I didn't want a big scene now. Obviously I had failed him when he needed me.

"What happened?" I asked for the 17 millionth time. I leaned against the counter; he leaned against the fridge.

"I didn't like us being separated," he said. "It stressed me out. I couldn't get a hold of you."

"But you knew where I was," I said. "You could have come over."

"Why? It seemed like you wanted me gone. You got all of your possessions out of our apartment when I wasn't there. It was as if we were breaking up."

Well, it did feel that way.

"Weren't we?" I asked. "I mean, you wanted to move back home."

"I wanted you to come with me," he said.

"Mark, we've had that conversation a thousand times," I said. "I wasn't going to move here. I wouldn't be happy here. It's too far from my kids."

"The beach was just as far," he said.

"But there was the beach," I said.

"And here there was me," he said. He shook his head. "You could never let go of the life you had with Hayword, no matter how messed up it was. You never even divorced him. How do you think that made me feel?"

"I thought you were over that," I said. "I thought we settled that years ago."

"You settled it by not talking about it," he said. "I was just supposed to accept it. Just like Hayword was supposed to accept you and me fucking. And you fucking everyone else under the sun."

"Hey," I said. "That is all water under the bridge."

"I need a meeting," he said.

"OK," I said. "We can talk about this later."

He looked at me. "I'm not blaming you," he said. "I was just trying to explain how I was feeling. Like I was never good enough for you, in your eyes."

"That's your shit," I said, "not mine."

"I took a drink yesterday," he said.

What the fuck was in the air yesterday that we both started drinking?

"Then Clare came over," he said. "And we had sex."

Clare. Who was Clare? Was that his ex-wife?

Mark was watching me. Did he want a reaction? Not want one? Was I relieved? Was I horrified? I didn't know. I felt so little. When had this started? When had I started feeling so little? Was there something wrong with me?

"I'm so sorry, Brooke," he said. "I know it's not an excuse, but I was drunk."

"Don't we do what we really want to do when we're drunk? It just gives us an excuse?"

He shook his head. "No. I wanted you. And then she was here."

"She was here?" I said. "So a woman showed up. She has the right orifices and you fuck her? Wow. I bet she'd be glad to hear that you fucked her because she was here."

"She was here," Mark said, "and she was listening to me. She was seeing me. She wanted to be with me."

OK. That was worse. He fucked her because she wasn't me and she showed up.

I wanted to scream, "Guess what, you cheating motherfucker: I was with Hayword yesterday. Sexually speaking. And then this morning, I fucked Ryan. So I've got you beat!"

But I didn't say it.

"Do you want me to look up some meeting times for you?" I asked.

Mark shook his head. "No, I know when and where to go. Will you come with me?"

Why did he ask me that? We never went to the same meetings together. Or rarely. Did he know I was drinking, too?

I wanted to say, "You stuck your dick into another woman. No, I don't want to go to an AA meeting with you."

"Did you at least use protection?" I asked. Pot calling the pan something or another.

"I don't know," he said. "I can't remember."

"Fuck," I said. "No, I'm not going to a fucking meeting with you. I'm sorry I didn't answer your phone calls or texts. But I can't be with you now. I can't help you through this. I thought you were the one person who would never betray me, and look what you've done."

"I didn't betray you," he said. "I had sex with another woman. I thought you didn't want me any more."

I stared at him. I wanted to feel something: love or hate or outrage. But I didn't feel anything.

"Maybe I don't want you any more," I said. "Especially now that you've got some other woman's cum all over your dick."

With those loving and caring words, I hurried out of the house. I got into my car and drove away. Only down the block. I stopped to make a few calls. Now I felt something. Now that I was away from him, I was angry.

Only I wasn't certain why.

I called our offices. Caryn, our receptionist slash secretary, answered.

"Hi, Caryn," I said. "Can you get me the home address of a Ryan Nichols? He should be in the Director's Directory."

"Sure," she said. "Sally said if you called she wanted you to call her."

"OK," I said. "Will you text me Ryan's address?"

"I will," she said. We ended the call.

I breathed deeply and then phoned Sally. When she answered, I said, "Are they giving us the money?"

"Yes," Sally said.

"So I saved the day."

"It didn't need saving until you started calling people names."

"He was wrong," I said.

"He's a stupid kid," Sally said. "A stupid rich kid. And there are some caveats on the investment."

"Like what?"

"They need to see some pages," Sally said.

"They are fucking children," I said. "They wouldn't know a good script if it hit them in the face."

"Let's not hit them with anything," Sally said. "They want to see some pages in a week. By next Monday."

"Even I'm not that fast."

Silence. And then, "Does that mean you don't have any pages done?"

Crap. "Um, no. I have pages. I have lots of pages. I've just got some personal stuff going on."

"You've always got something going on, Mac," she said. "What is it now?"

"Don't talk to me like I'm two years old," I said.

"You've had two years to write this fucking thing," Sally said.

"Mark cheated on me," I said. OK. That wasn't what was causing me stress or a delay in the manuscript, but I wasn't going to tell her I was drinking. Or had drunk. Drank?

"That sucks," Sally said. "I'm sorry to hear that. What are you gonna do? If Jonathan cheated on me, I would kill him and the bitch he cheated with." She sounded angry.

"Guess you've thought about this," I said.

"Lately he's seemed so distance," Sally said, "so I've been wondering if he's cheating. Been thinking about what I'd do. When I think about everything I've given up to have this family."

"You mean like fucking me?"

Sally laughed. "We were over long before Jonathan. Besides, you told me I was a pain in the ass."

"It's true," I said. "In general women are more of a pain in the ass than men. Thank god I never fucked Joanie. You wouldn't believe the mess she's gotten herself into."

"Do tell."

Oh shit. It was a secret.

"I better wait," I said. "I'll tell you when I know more."

"There's something else the boys want," Sally said. "Damon wants Fern to be involved with the project."

"You want me to pimp out my daughter to get this investment?"

"Of course not," Sally said. "But she's closer to their age, and Damon likes her. What could it hurt? She does work for the company. Why not?"

"It's up to her," I said. "But what do you know about them? Are they drinkers? Druggies? Misogynists?"

"Do you know the answers to those questions for everyone your daughter dates?"

"Dates? I thought she was going to be *working* with them. If they are working together, they cannot date until the project is finished. Make sure that's clear."

"All right," Sally said. "Jesus. But we start filming in a month. If I don't have the script by next Monday, we will have to hire someone else, and we'll lose these investors."

"You can't do that," I said. "I'm part owner, and I have to agree to that. And I don't."

"Just write the fucking script!" Sally said. She sounded angry again. Why did everyone sound so angry with me?

Because everyone was angry with me.

"Fuck off," I said.

And that was the end of the phone call. Just then, Caryn sent me a text: Ryan Nichols' address. He still lived close to Mark.

I put the address into my GPS and headed out.

I didn't know what I was going to do when I got to his house. I felt out of control and peaceful and horrible all at the same time. It was as if I had been tied up in knots for years, and now I was coming . . . undone.

A few blocks and a few minutes later, I was walking up the sidewalk to Ryan's nondescript one-story ranch house. When I got to the door, I rang the bell. Ryan answered. He looked surprised to see me. Or shocked. Or afraid. He also looked drunk.

I said, "You promised that we would be together forever."

He took a deep breath. "I obviously didn't mean it."

"I was in such grief when you left," I said. "I'm sure that grief affected Alberto. I'm sure that stress contributed to his death from SIDS."

"So you're saying I'm the reason our son died?"

I felt a twinge of fury. (Can one have a twinge of fury?) How dare he call Alberto *our* son.

"Yes, I am blaming you," I said.

"What can I do about it now?" he asked.

"Nothing," I answered. "Just don't do it to anyone else, ever again."

"I was young and stupid," he said. "And I was afraid. I didn't know anything about raising a kid."

"So you just left?"

"It was a complete asshole move," he said. "Do you want to come in for a beer?"

I shook my head. "I'll go to a meeting with you."

"I've already been," he said. "It didn't help."

"It doesn't work that way," I said.

"How would you know?"

"You got coffee?" I asked.

He nodded, moved out of the way, and I stepped into Ryan Nichols' house. I followed him into the kitchen. Somehow we bumped into each other. We started kissing again.

I pulled away and asked, "Do you have any chocolate?"

"No."

I shrugged. "OK. I guess we better fuck then."

And that's what I did for the rest of the afternoon: Alberto's baby daddy and I had sex. Several times. Apparently I had actually cured him of impotence by getting him to drink. Or something. Neither of us drank anything, but he went into the bathroom a couple of times and came out happy. I figured he was taking something.

"Let's not use protection this time," he said mid-afternoon. "We can make another baby, to make up for what happened to Alberto."

"You don't trade dead children for living children," I said. "That's disgusting."

"That's not what I'm saying. We could have another one. And do right by it. I wouldn't leave this time."

I laughed, grabbed my shirt by the bed and put it on. "And what, we'd live here and live happily ever after? I am not that woman you left behind a decade and a half ago. I am meaner and leaner."

"Obviously," Ryan said. "I don't care."

"You don't want to have a baby with me," I said. "You don't know me. You're just higher than a kite."

"I know," he said. "But I can fuck like a stud again. It's great. You ready to go again?"

"I have to get a drink." I got out of bed and stumbled to the kitchen, half-dressed. I looked around for some liquor and found an open bottle of vodka. I took a gulp. I loved the way it burned my throat. I hurried down the hall again. Ryan came out of the bedroom and pushed me gently up against the wall.

"Here," he said. "For old time's sake."

"Fucking standing up or against a wall?" I said.

"Both," he said.

He picked me up by my thighs. I put my arms around his neck as he maneuvered his penis into my vagina. I loved feeling the wall against my back, Ryan's dick inside me, the vodka in my belly. I moaned with pleasure.

Then something turned. In my stomach. "Oh no," I said, a second before I vomited all over Ryan. Yep. Right in his face and on his bare chest.

He screamed and dropped me. Fortunately, I landed on my feet, and I ran to the bathroom. Where I threw up again.

I heard Ryan in the hallway. "What the fuck?" he was saying.

I wiped my mouth and stood. I reeked. I turned the water on in the shower and stepped into it. I let the water run over me, washing away all the vomit and all the sin. I didn't know why I threw up. Maybe I had developed an allergy to vodka?

I came out of the bathroom, all dry and clean, as Ryan was walking down the hall toward me. He was dressed. He must have showered, too.

"Sorry about that," I said. "You might have a bad batch of vodka."

"This is certainly your day for revenge," he said. "You got me to drink again, and then you vomited all over me while we were having sex. I don't know how much worse this day can get."

I laughed. What an asshole he was. Why had I come here?

"I'm sorry for what I did to you all those years ago," he said. "I'm sorry about Alberto. But this, whatever this is, is crazy. I need to go to a meeting."

I suddenly felt very naked. I took the towel off my head and wrapped it around my body.

"There's a meeting down the street in about 15 minutes," he said. "I'm going. Do you want to come?"

"Sure," I said. "Text me the address, and I'll meet you there. I need to get dressed."

"OK. Lock the door when you leave."

Then he was gone, out of sight. I heard the front door open and close. I went to the bedroom, retrieved my clothes, and got dressed. My stomach still felt strange. I needed something to eat. I opened Ryan's fridge. It was nearly empty except for some cold cuts. From Ruby's. Very expensive. She made great bread, too. I looked around the kitchen until I found half a loaf of her Como bread. Also expensive. I made a sandwich and ate a few delicious bites. I put half of it in my purse. I dropped the partially-eaten half into the sink, where Ryan would see it.

Then I took some red lipstick from the bottom of my purse. I pulled the top off as I stood in the living room looking around.

I turned the lipstick so it was all the way up. I liked the color scheme in Ryan's house. One living room wall was dark turquoise. I stood on his couch and leaned forward. Then, using my lipstick as a pen, I wrote on his wall in big capital letters "LOSER." I turned the lipstick back down, put the top on again, and dropped it on the couch. The lipstick was contaminated now. I wouldn't use it again. I supposed my vagina was contaminated now, too, again, with Ryan cooties.

Oh well. I wasn't leaving that behind.

I left the house and drove away.

CHAPTER SIX

I drove right by Mark's house. I thought about stopping to see if he was all right. His truck was there. But I kept going. My phone rang soon after. I pulled over to the side of the road.

It was David.

"Mom," he said. "Where are you? You were supposed to pick me up from school."

"What? Why?" We had bought him a car as soon as he got his license so that we wouldn't have to be there to pick him up.

"The car is in the shop," he said. "Dad reminded you."

Shit. He had reminded me.

"I'm sorry," I said. "I had a meeting downtown, and I forgot. I'm still in the city. I'll never get there in time. Aren't you there kind of late?"

"I had my climate change study group," he said. "Do you ever listen to a fucking thing I say?"

"David," I said. "Language, please. I'm sorry. I'll call your dad and see if he is at the house."

"Don't bother," David said. "I'll do it." And the call ended.

"He fucking hung up on me," I said. "That little shit."

I had always liked David. Of course I loved all three of my children. Alberto never got old enough for me to dislike him. But Fern had. I did not like her. We had our moments over the years where it seemed like we had reached a rapprochement. Then something would happen or the winds would shift, and she hated me all over again. I still loved her, but who wants to be around someone who is so disagreeable all the time?

David had always been agreeable until now. He had been worried most of his life about something. He was afraid. He had lots of anxiety. But he liked me. He never hated me. He never accused me of ruining his life. Fern had accused me of ruining her life since she first became a teenager. Now that she was grown up, in her twenties, working a real job her mother and father got her, she was still testy. Now David was apparently following in her footsteps. I did not like that.

I called David. He answered with, "What?"

"Listen, David," I said. "I am sorry I didn't pick you up. But that's no reason to act like a little shit. I get enough of that crap from your sister. You speak to me respectfully or don't speak to me at all."

"You mean I have that choice?" he said.

Little fucker.

"What could I have possibly done to make you so angry with me?" I asked. "We had a great relationship and then suddenly the past few months, you've been treating me like crap."

"I suppose you're going to use that as an excuse for why you started drinking?" He said it combatively, but I could hear the fear hidden behind the words. He was worried he had caused my relapse.

Maybe I could use his treatment of me as an excuse for my drinking.

Jesus.

No, no. Through it all, I had been a good mother. I never let them know how I was really feeling. Never let them know how drunk I was. I was a good mother no matter what. Right? That was a good thing, not telling them anything about how I felt or what I was going through. Besides, I was a drunk ages ago; I had been sober for years now.

"No," I said. "And I'm not drinking." Not now. Hadn't had a drink in hours. OK, I had had a drink, but I had vomited it all up. "Besides, I wouldn't blame you for my drinking."

"See, you're still lying," David said. "I know about all the men you slept with when you were a drunk."

All the men *and* women. I thought he already knew that. Hadn't we talked about it?

"You cheated on Dad over and over," he said. "It wasn't just Alberto's father."

"That was so long ago," I said. "I'm a different person. I've made amends."

"You haven't made amends to us," David said. "I don't remember you ever making amends to the family."

"I did," I said. "I'm sorry if you don't remember, but I apologized to all three of you. Why is this coming up now?"

"Because I know now what you did," David said. "And I can't believe Dad just forgave you and now you're sleeping together again."

"Who is telling you all of this?" I asked.

"It doesn't matter," he said.

"It most certainly does matter," I said. "Who is saying these things to you?"

It had to be Fern or Hayword. Hayword was the only other person who knew we had had sex.

"Your father should not be talking to you about these kinds of things," I said.

"It's not Dad," David said. "I found a site on the dark web. It's called the Whore of Hollywood, and it has a list of all the people you've had sex with."

"What?" I said. Oh my gawd. This couldn't be true. No, no, calm down, calm down. No one in the world knew everyone I had had sex with. Not even me. I certainly had never written anything down.

"Are there pictures?" I blurted out.

"No!" David said.

"You believed something on the dark web?" I said. "Why didn't you just ask me about it?"

"How could I ask my mother if she is a whore?"

"For one thing, you would never ask that of anyone. That's a derogatory term usually used against women."

"Men can be whores, too," he said.

"The word comes from the Horae, or hours," I said. "The Horae were sacred priestesses who knew the mysteries of sex and helped teach men about them so they would be better lovers."

"Is that what you were doing?" David sounded disgusted.

"No," I said. "The point isn't what I was or wasn't doing. Whore is now a misogynist term used against women to try to take our power away. Send me the link. Or whatever it is you do to get on the dark web. I need to figure this out."

"Does that mean you didn't cheat on Dad?" David asked.

"That's a complex question," I said. "You know that Dad wasn't Alberto's biological father."

"Yeah," he said, "but I thought he was the only one."

"It's really none of your business."

"That means yes, you cheated on Dad."

"That means it's none of your fucking business!" I said. "Do you want me to call a car service for you or can you find a way home?"

"I'll find a way," he said.

I immediately called Hayword. I was surprised when he answered.

"I was supposed to pick up David," I said. "But I forgot. Are you at the house? Can you pick him up?"

"Where have you been all afternoon?" he asked. "Did you find another old beau to fuck today?"

I gasped. How could he know? He couldn't, he couldn't. He was just being mean.

"I was at a meeting," I said.

"Which one?" He didn't believe me.

"Can you pick him up or not?"

"I can and I will."

I ended the call. I looked at the clock. If I got on the freeway now it would be hours until I got home. I hung my head. I was closer to the studio, traffic-wise. Maybe someone was still there who could help me with this Whore of Hollywood website. I glanced at my phone. David had sent me a link. I didn't dare look at it.

It took me a while to get to our offices, but finally I drove into the lovely complex of old bungalows that were now offices, mostly for movie people. We called our offices a studio, but we didn't actually have any places to make movies, not like the old MGM studios: We just had offices. When we made a movie, we were mostly on location.

I used my key to go through the front door of Back to Life Studios. Caryn was still at her desk, but the doors were locked. She smiled when she saw me. "You decided to avoid the traffic, too," she said.

I nodded. "It's been a clusterfuck day," I said. "Hey, Caryn, is there anyone here who could help me get onto the dark web? Is that what it's called?"

"I could," she said. "I keep an eye on it in case anyone is

saying bad things about our actors or directors. I have an anonymizing tool on my computer. It's part of my job."

"Oh," I said. "I had no idea." I really was fairly ignorant about our operations. Why was that?

"I'm sorry I didn't know that," I said. I showed her my phone. "My son says there's a website there called the Whore of Hollywood, and it's all about me. It has a list of people I've had sex with. Although that's impossible. I mean, it can't be true. But I need to see it."

"Sure," Caryn said. "It'll take me a minute."

I nodded. "Thanks. I'll go to my office," I said. "Haven't been there in a while."

I walked down the narrow hall. I liked the light yellow walls and the prints of flowers and beaches penned in by tasteful frames. It was all lovely and soothing. My office was decorated in pastels. I only had one painting on one wall: It was a colored egg with a deep blue background. The name of the painting was Creation.

I glanced out the window. Darkness was falling.

I sat at my desk and smoothed my hand across the wooden top. It was such a lovely desk. Why didn't I ever come here?

"It's nice, isn't it?"

I looked up. My daughter was standing in the doorway.

"Hello, Fern," I said. "I didn't know you were here."

"And I didn't know you were here," she said. "May I come in?"

"Of course," I said.

She was holding a file folder. She stepped into the office and closed the door. She then closed the blinds so no one from the hallway could see us.

"We don't bug our offices, do we?" she asked as she sat in the chair on the other side of my beautiful wooden desk.

"Not that I know about," I said.

She was being quite pleasant, but she usually was at the office. I will give her that: She was professional.

"Mom, I tried to take care of this myself," she said. "But I haven't been able to. I apologize for bringing it to you, but you're the only one I can trust. You're the only one who will understand."

"Uh-oh," I said. "This doesn't sound good. You're buttering me up."

"I'm being blackmailed," she said. "They're telling me that they will publish these photos if I don't pay them a million dollars."

"What?" Was this a joke?

"Is this another one of your pranks?" I asked.

She frowned.

"Like the staged robbery in the restaurant?"

She shook her head. "No, Mom. I'm having an affair with a married man. I love him. He's promised to leave his wife. But if she finds out now, it could ruin everything, for all of us."

"For all of us?" I asked.

She put the folder on the desk and pushed it toward me. I did not want to open it. Did not want to see my daughter having sex.

I sighed and opened the folder. There in living color was my daughter, naked, astride a man's lap. The man's face was scrunched up in passion, I supposed, although he looked like he was taking a shit. The man was Jonathan, the husband of Sally St. James.

"Fuck," I said. "You've really screwed the pooch this time, sister."

CHAPTER SEVEN

"Who is blackmailing you?" I asked.

"I don't know," Fern said. "The photos just showed up on my desk."

"So someone in our company is blackmailing you?"

"I don't think so," Fern said. "There was a postmark. Later I got a text. I know I screwed up. But what do I do now? I don't have a million dollars." She looked at me.

"You think I have a million dollars just in my wallet for the taking?" I asked.

"If these get published in a tabloid, our company will be ruined."

"Sally will kill you," I said. "She suspects Jonathan is cheating, and she said she would kill him and the bitch who was sleeping with him. That's a quote."

Fern squirmed in her chair. "That's just something people say. She wouldn't really hurt me. People don't kill other people because of an affair."

I raised an eyebrow. "Apparently you don't watch a lot of TV. Of course people kill each other over shit like this."

"Mom, you're scaring me."

"You should be fucking scared," I said. "You come in here all calm, asking your rich momma to bail you out. How could you sleep with Sally's husband? That's a horrible betrayal."

Fern's eyes widened. "You are talking to me about betrayal? How many husbands did you fuck?"

"None," I said. "Except my own. I would never do that to another woman."

"I don't believe you," she said. "I've seen the list. Some of those men were married."

I slapped my hand on the desk. "It was you who told David."

She shook her head. "David told me about the list, and I checked it out."

"Did you talk to him about the list?"

"You mean about your former sex life?" Fern said. "No! That's not a conversation I want to have with anyone, especially not with my little brother."

"I don't believe you," I said. "He's been treating me like shit for months now, and I knew someone must be poisoning him with bad mommy stories."

"He's got his own bad mommy stories," Fern said, "from all the years you lived with us when you were drunk on your ass and fucking everyone but daddy dearest."

I sucked in a breath and got to my feet. I had never wanted to hit one of my children more than I did at that moment.

"I am not giving you a million fucking dollars," I said. "Or even a penny. Sally won't split up the company for this. But we will fire you for it. So good luck. Now get out of my office."

Fern got to her feet, snatched the file from my desk, opened the door and left. She tried to slam the door, but is was partially pneumatic or something. But she was gone. I stared after her.

That conversation had been mildly satisfying. I had always wanted to say, "Get out of my office." Like in the movies. Or on TV. Now I had.

I was as bad as all of them. All of them who loved this cesspool called Hollywood. I had been sucked in. I had been enjoying myself for the last few years, because of the success of *Beauty and the Zombie*. It had been fun to be rich and semi-famous and sober. I rubbed my head. None of it was real. We made these ridiculous movies while the world fell down around us. Only the disasters reminded us that it was all going to hell in a handbasket: the earthquakes, fires, floods, viruses. No disasters now to blame anything on, no disasters to finally wake us up. Just me drinking. And now Fern fucking her boss's husband.

I sat down again. I really couldn't let those photos get out.

There was a knock at the door. I heard Caryn's voice. I told her to come in. She walked in carrying her laptop which she put on my desk. The screen was covered in a kind of dark purple with the words "Whore of Hollywood" scrawled across it in the same font as the *Beauty and the Zombie* title credits. I leaned forward. In white letters below the Whore of Hollywood I read, "Brooke McMurphy pretends she is the perfect mother and wife, but those in the know know that she has slept with more men than the whore of Babylon. She's ruined many marriages. Was yours one? Here's the list."

I blinked, and the afterimages stayed. "White lettering on a dark background. Amateur shit. And I slept with just as many women as men. Well, OK, not quite as many."

I looked up at Caryn. She smiled wanly. "Sorry," I said, "but accuracy is important in these things."

"Certainly."

I leaned closer to read the list of names and squinted. Yes, him. Yes, him. No, not him. No, gawd, no, not him no matter how drunk I was. Ryan Nichols' name was there. All in all, I read about 30 names. Most of them I knew. About half of them I had probably had sex with during those years when I was a drunk.

"Thank you, Caryn," I said. "Is there any way you can find out who put this up? Can we get it taken down?"

She shook her head. "I doubt it. I can do some searching though, bring in some of my buddies, if this is important to you. But no one will see this, most likely. If it's not true, who cares?"

"My children have seen it," I said, "and there's enough truth to it that they believe it." I looked up at her. "I used to be a drunk."

Caryn nodded. "Been there, done that. I've been sober for three years."

I smiled. "Congratulations." I figured she wanted me to say how long I had been sober, but I didn't want to tell anyone else that I had started drinking. Why confess to a lapse? I wasn't drinking *now*. I wouldn't drink any more. There. I had decided. No more drinking.

"Yes, do whatever you can to find out who put it up," I said. "If you can get it gone, that would be great."

"If we find out who it is," Caryn said, "we can threaten legal action. Sometimes that's enough."

"Great," I said. "Thank you. Keep this between us and your crew for now. I want to see if I can keep it quiet."

"Of course." Caryn took her laptop and left the office, letting the door close softly behind her.

Now what? I needed to find out who was blackmailing Fern. Phil Case, our old friend who had worked Major Crimes for many years in Los Angeles, had retired last year and set up shop as a private investigator. He had pulled our familial bacon out of the fire more than once. Maybe he could do it again.

I left my office—phone in hand—and walked down the hall

to Fern's office. The door was open. She was sitting on her couch, texting.

"Texting your lover?" I asked.

She looked up at me. "Shhh," she said. "You don't know who's here."

I rolled my eyes and shut the door.

"Did you tell Jonathan?" I asked.

She shook her head.

"It's not him blackmailing us is it?" I asked. Fern had a bit of a history with boyfriends using her to get to us.

"No," she said. "He is successful businessman."

"He's got kids, you know," I said.

"So did you," she said.

I sighed. "No one broke up my marriage with your father."

"Ryan Nichols did," she said.

I had never heard her say his name out loud, at least not since I told her about him a few years earlier.

"He didn't," I said. "Your father and I stayed together to raise our family. We loved each other. We still love each other."

She made a noise.

I sighed. "Why do we always have to go over old ground? It's in the past. All of this."

"Why do you still mourn Alberto?" she asked.

"That feels like a particularly nasty question," I said.

"I don't mean it that way," Fern said. "You want to know why I keep bringing up the past. Alberto is in the past, and you still mourn him."

I leaned against the wall. "OK. I'll give you that. But you're still so angry about things that happened years ago. You blame me for everything bad in your life. You've got to take responsibility for your life. My parents were clueless, but I know they did the best they could."

"You did not do the best you could," Fern said. "As a mother."

"And as a daughter, you haven't done the best you could either," I said. I put up a hand and shook my head. "I'm not going to do this with you. I'm going to call Phil Case and see if he can figure out who is blackmailing you."

"But then other people will know," Fern said. "Please don't tell Dad. I don't want him to know."

"People are going to know," I said. "It's a crime to blackmail someone."

"I just want to pay it," Fern said. "And get the photos back."

"Back from where?" I asked. "If the photos are online, they are there forever. Maybe if we find the guy, though, we can get him prosecuted."

"I don't want Jonathan to know about it," Fern said. "I love him, Mom."

She looked at me with pathetic puppy dog eyes. Good grief. She was too young to be that madly in love. Of course, I had been younger than she was when Hayword and I got together. I don't think I was ever madly in love with him, though. Not crazy, like I had been with Ryan. Thank goodness. How can you build a life when you're sick with love all the time? I shuddered.

"He will leave me if this comes out," Fern said. "And he can't go through a divorce right now. They have a prenup."

"What does that matter if they're both rich?" I asked. "Or if he's so in love with you."

Fern shrugged.

"How long has this been going on?" I asked.

"Six months," she said.

"And the blackmail?"

"About two months ago," she said.

"And you're just taking care of it now?"

"I was stalling for time," she said. "I paid him a little here and there. But then he texted me that he wanted the money this week or he was going to the tabloids."

"Six months," I said. "Jesus, Fern. He's old enough to be your father. He has children."

"You already said that!" Fern said. "I'm hoping to have my children with him."

"Are you pregnant?" I asked.

"No," she said. "Not yet."

I wanted to shake her.

"You are a talented woman," I said. "You're interesting and beautiful. There are unmarried men out there who would love to spend time with you. Just today Damon Friend said he wants you to be part of the *Beauty and the Zombie Part Three* team."

"That's work," she said. "And I'm already a part of that team. Have you finished the script? Does Aiden come back from the dead?"

I wished people would quit asking me that question.

"I'm just saying that you don't need this guy. It's beneath you to be doing this. You're a modern woman. Be your own person with or without a significant other."

"Like you?" Fern asked. "You were going to leave us for Ryan Nichols."

"No," I said. "I was willing to leave Hayword, not you or David. You would have come with me."

Fern laughed. "Never. We would have never left Dad."

I stared at her. She looked me right in the eyes.

I nodded. She was right. The kids would not have left Hayword.

"Besides," she said. "We were a unit, the four of us and then the five of us. If you left one of us, you left all of us."

"And now that's what you want Jonathan to do," I said. "You want him to break up the family unit."

"Sally already did that by being a bitch," Fern said.

"Oh, Jesus H. Christ," I said. "You fell for that old saw? I taught you better than that."

"No, you didn't!" She was standing now and yelling. "You taught me how to be a drunk and a whore."

That's when I slapped my daughter across the face. Hard. It left a red mark.

"Don't you ever talk to me like that again," I said.

We stood a few feet from one another, breathing hard. Tears flooded her eyes, and she looked like she wanted to kill me. I'm sure I looked the same. I couldn't believe I had hit her. Given all the other things I had done that day, I shouldn't have been surprised.

"I'm going to call Phil Case now and see if he can clean up another one of your fuck-ups, daughter dearest."

I left her office. I felt like I was going to throw up. I wondered if this was some weird hangover or was my body feeling something I wasn't willing to process: sex with my ex, finding a dead body, sex with another ex, not sex with another ex who was now drinking, realizing I had forgotten my dead son's birthday, finding out my daughter was having sex with someone else's soon to be ex, and hitting my daughter. Good grief.

Once in my office, I curled up in one of my cushy chairs and phoned Phil Case. I was surprised when he answered.

"Hi, Phil. It's Brooke McMurphy. Long time."

"Hi, Mac. What did you do now?"

"Funny shit, Phil. It's not me. I want to hire you. You keep everything private, right?"

"Sure," he said, "unless I get called to court and then all bets are off."

"I don't think this will go to court," I said. "My daughter is being blackmailed. They've got what you might call compromising photos."

"Like what?" Phil asked. "Speeding? Killing someone? Fucking someone?"

"The latter," I said. "And she's fucking someone she shouldn't be."

"Like the boss?"

"Like the boss's husband," I said.

"That's not good," he said.

"It would not be good for the studio if these got out."

"Where are you?" he asked.

"I'm at the Back to Life offices," I said. "Where are you?"

"I'm downtown," he said. "I can drop by now. Be there in ten."

"OK. I'll let you in."

I went out to reception. It was dark. Caryn must have gone home.

I walked to the kitchen and searched the cupboards for something to drink. I didn't find anything besides tea and coffee—and a chocolate bar. I unwrapped the bar and ate it in about ten seconds flat.

I went to reception and sat in Caryn's chair. It was dark outside now, twilight. Not my favorite time of the day. I hadn't seen Phil for a while. I liked him. Didn't think he liked me. He was a good-looking man. Kept himself in shape. At least he did when he was on the job. Not sure about now. But he was married. So that was out. Why was I even thinking about him in that way? How many times had I had sex today? Had I become some kind of nymphomaniac over night?

Suddenly Phil was there, outside. He smiled, and I got up and unlocked the door, and he came inside. He looked even better than the last time I had seen him. I locked the door again, and we embraced. I probably held on a little longer than I should have. I had to get a hold of myself.

"Hi, Phil," I said. "How's retirement treating you?"

"My wife left me, and my kids hate me," he said. "Other than that, it's all good."

"Oh, shit," I said. "That sucks. I thought you two were the perfect married couple."

We started to walk down the semi-dark hall.

"Why would you say that?"

I shrugged. "I guess because you weren't divorced."

"Then you and Hayword must be the perfect couple since you're not divorced."

"Shut up," I said. We passed my office and went to Fern's. Her light was on. She was sitting on the couch, still, only this time she had a drink on the table in front of her. Looked like some kind of hard liquor.

She no longer had a red spot on her cheek. I flinched slightly, thinking about it. I hoped this day would end without me killing anyone or ruining anyone else's life. Fern stood and held her hand out to Phil.

"Hello, Mr. Case," she said. They shook hands.

"Please sit," I said.

Phil sat on the couch next to Fern. I sat in the chair. We all stared at the folder on the coffee table.

"Do you really have to look at those?" Fern asked. "It's so embarrassing."

Phil said, "It's possible I can tell something about the person blackmailing you from looking at them. What kind of photos are they. Professional. Amateur. From a phone or a camera. Where they were taken. I've seen a million crime photos. These won't bother me."

"At least these aren't photos of dead people," I said. I didn't know where that came from. They both looked at me and then away.

"Where were you?" Phil asked.

"Just some hotel," Fern said, "that Jonathan found. I can get you the name."

"And the curtains or blinds were open?" Phil asked.

"They must have been," Fern said. "I didn't even think about it. We were six stories up."

Phil nodded. I rolled my eyes. First rule of having illicit sex: Close the fucking curtains.

"Do you remember what was across the street?" Phil asked. "An apartment building? A hotel?"

Fern shrugged. "I don't know. I wasn't paying attention."

Second rule of having illicit sex: Pay attention to your surroundings. I should write a book: *How to Have Illicit Sex and Get Away With It.*

"OK," Phil said. "Are you ready to show me?"

"Do I have to stay and watch you look at naked photos of me?" Fern asked.

"Yes," I said "If I have to stay, you do, too."

"I'm not a child," Fern said. "You can't tell me what to do."

"I might have questions," Phil said. He picked up the file folder and began flipping through the photos. It didn't take long. Then he shut the folder.

"May I see what he said when he contacted you?"

Fern picked up her phone, scrolled at bit, and then handed it to Phil. He wrote down something and then handed it back to her. He asked her the name of the hotel, the date they were there, and the room number. She told him.

"I can't tell you anything for certain," Phil said. "I need to do some investigating, but I'm pretty sure you were targeted. These look professional to me. My guess is that it's a paparazzi. Have you had run-ins with any pap in particular?"

"I don't think I'd know one if I saw one," Fern said.

"Any reporters?"

"No," Fern said. "I don't think so."

"How about you, Mac?"

"Me? No. I ignore the paparazzi. When I got out of rehab a few years ago, they covered me, but that's about it."

"What about the new movie?" he said. "I've been hearing rumblings that it's about to start and there's no script."

"What would that have to do with anything?" I asked.

"Maybe the studio is trying to create buzz with a scandal?"

"Hayward and I and Sally are the studio," I said. "We don't want anything like this out."

"OK," Phil said. "Let me run some things down. Fern, I'd advise you to tell your gentleman friend what's going on. See if anyone has been after him."

"I don't want to tell him," Fern said.

"It's probably going to come out one way or another," Phil said. "That's the way these things are."

Fern looked terrified. "I need to get going," she said. She picked up the folder and grabbed her purse. Phil and I got up and left the office. Fern followed us out and locked her door.

"Keep in touch," I told Fern. She didn't say anything. She just hurried by us.

Phil and I went to my office. "You want me to get you some water or coffee?" I asked. "I could probably scrounge some up."

"Naw," he said. "I better get on this. The guy wants an answer by this week or he's going to publish. My guess is that he's a paparazzi just trying to make some extra dough before he turns over the photos. They're going to get published one way or another. At least that's my guess."

"Can't you find out who it is," I asked, "and then go intimidate him?"

"Blackmail is illegal," he said, "but taking and selling photos isn't. I'll try to find out who he is. Maybe you can threaten legal action."

"That's the second time I've been given that advice today,"

I said. I sat on the couch. Phil sat in the chair kitty-corner from me.

"Oh?"

"There's a website on the dark web that purports to be a list of all the men I've had sex with," I said. "It's call the Whore of Hollywood."

"Ouch," Phil said. "That doesn't sound good. Is it real?"

"You mean the list?" I shook my head. "No, it's not. But my kids believe it's real. When I was drinking my appetite for all things was voracious."

Phil nodded. "I remember."

"What do you mean you remember?"

"Hayword had to talk to someone," he said.

"Jesus," I said. "And to think I was going to try to seduce you. Now I just feel icky."

Phil laughed.

He thought I was kidding.

"Have you talked to Hayword lately?" I asked.

"A couple weeks ago," he said. "He was dating someone. Really liked her." Phil looked at me.

I said, "Don't say anything to Hayword about this. I'll tell him when it's time."

"You're my client," Phil said. "I can keep my mouth shut."

"You want to go have dinner? The traffic will still be too bad to go home."

Phil said, "Sure. But don't make any moves on me. I'm weak. My wife left me for a younger man. Any attention is quite gratifying."

We both stood. "I won't make any promises," I said.

CHAPTER EIGHT

It was good having a nice normal dinner with someone outside the business and not part of my family. Phil talked about missing his old life. I talked about missing a time in my life when I was relaxed. Although I couldn't remember when that was.

I didn't drink. I didn't try to seduce him. I went home alone to my dark bungalow, took off my clothes, and crawled into bed. I hoped I would wake up and this was all a dream.

I dreamed of Alberto. He was far away and waving to me, waving me toward him.

When I woke up, my heart was racing. Was Alberto telling me to come toward him, toward death? Because that was where he was. He was dead.

I shuddered. It was daylight. I had made it through the night. I remembered the vodka bottle was still in the cupboard. I longed for a swig, but I stayed away from the cupboard. I got dressed. Then I scrambled a couple of eggs and ate them with bacon and toast. I felt like shit.

I sat at the table looking out at my backyard. What was happening to me? Why had I suddenly gone off the deep end? Was it the fact that no one in my family seemed to want anything to do with me? Now I knew why: They were mad at me over the Whore of Hollywood list. And currently, no doubt, Fern was mad at me for hitting her. She had a right. I should have never done that. Bleck. What now? I wished I believed in therapy, because I could use a good shrink. Or a good drink.

It wasn't that I didn't believe in therapy; it was just that it never worked for me. Yes, I drank because my kid died. And I fucked around because my kid died, and I was mad at Hayword because he cheated on me. And yes, I couldn't seem to move out of that hole of grief. Until I did. I went to rehab, and I hadn't had a drink since, not through two successful movies, not through my make up and break up and make up with Mark. Not through the earthquakes and floods and fires. Not through finding a dead guy right in this living room.

I was going in circles. This was not productive. I could figure this out. I could stop it. I could stop drinking and fucking.

The doorbell rang.

Crap.

If someone was selling me religion, I would slap them across the face, too.

"Brooke!"

It was Sally. Oh fuck, oh fuck, oh fuck. Had she found out about Jonathan and Fern?

"I'll be right there," I said. I glanced around the place. No sign that I had been drinking yesterday. I opened the door. Sally strode in, tall, thin, and so white—and gorgeous, as usual.

"I brought croissants," she said. She walked to the kitchen in two strides. "Unless you're not eating gluten or butter. I can't keep up with everyone these days."

"There's strawberry jam in the fridge," I said.

"No need," Sally said. "The croissants are filled with chocolate. Mine's filled with chocolate and vodka." She took down two small plates and put two croissants down on each. "This is mine," she said pointing to the right plate. "I need to wash up. You have coffee?"

She swooped into the bathroom. As soon as she was out of sight, I switched the right plate with the left one. Then I poured her a cup of coffee. I picked up the left plate (the former right one) and returned to the table. I wanted the vodka-laced croissant.

Sally came out of the bathroom. She looked at the remaining plate. "Did you take the right one?" she asked.

"I took the correct one, yes. And there's your coffee."

Sally brought her plate and coffee over to the table. I bit into the croissant. All that doughy goodness, all that butter and chocolate. Where was the vodka? I couldn't taste it. I took several bites as we stared out the window together.

"Was there really vodka in yours?" I asked.

"No, and there isn't any in yours," Sally said. "I wanted to see if you'd switch plates, and you did. I put a tiny smear of chocolate on mine. See." She pointed. "If you'd been smart, you would have changed the croissants, not the plates."

"What the fuck?" I asked.

"I wanted to see if you were drinking," Sally said.

"You could have asked."

"Are you drinking?"

"None of your business," I said.

"See," she said. "There's no vodka in anything. What can I do to help? Is it bad? Do you need to go into rehab?"

She was being awfully nice.

"No," I said. "I've got it under control."

Sally raised an eyebrow. "We could fuck. Would that help?"

I looked at her. "How would that help?"

"I dunno," she said. "I'm just so good that you would be cured of all that ails you."

I laughed. "I don't know what ails me. Brain chemistry. I still don't understand why I did it." I put my head in my hands. "And then Hayword and I had sex."

"Oh lordy," Sally said.

"And then I went to Ryan's AA meeting," I said. "And we had sex. Many, many times. Until I threw up on him."

"Oh my word!"

"In-between all that, I learned that Mark had cheated on me," I said.

"Did he cheat before or after you cheated on him?" Sally asked.

"What does that matter?" I said. "He cheated first. But I haven't been around. We have barely seen each other for weeks. We haven't had sex for weeks and weeks. I mean, not that that's everything. But for us, it was a way we got close. I started wondering why we were even together. It was so boring out there on the beach. But back here, with Hayword and the kids, it reminded me of the old days when I was drinking and carrying on. I missed it."

"Not really," Sally said.

I looked at her. "I missed people wanting me and wanting to be around me. It feels like the world is ending and everyone is mad at me."

"The world is ending," Sally said. "It's always ending."

"But this feels so big," I said, "and David keeps asking me why we didn't stop climate change when we could. I don't have answers for him. And there was David liking Hayword's new girlfriend. There was Hayword liking his new girlfriend. I thought what about me, even though I don't think I really thought that. But, maybe. Then I took that drink."

"You took that drink so it could be all about you again."

I stared at her. Oh, fuck. Was that it?

"Maybe," I said. "I dunno."

"How about we take your mind off of all of that?"

"I like the idea of fucking," I said.

Sally smiled. "It would be a pity fuck," she said. "Besides, I'm still hoping Jonathan and I can work on our marriage."

Her marriage. Christ. I had forgotten about that.

"I hope so," I said.

"Maybe working on the script would help you," Sally said.

I nodded. "OK. You run along, and I will do that."

Sally laughed. "Let's do it together. Come on. Get your laptop. We can brainstorm."

"Let me finish these delicious non-alcoholic croissants first," I said.

"Stalling," she said.

We talked and ate and drank coffee. Eventually I went to the couch, and she sat in the chair. I sat cross-legged and took my laptop from the coffee table and put it on the cushion in front of me. I wondered how long I could pretend that I had pages.

"Do you want to read me what you have?" Sally asked.

I shook my head.

"I assume the first shot is of Aiden's arm coming out of the grave?"

"We see Molly walking away from Aiden's gravesite," I said, "and Colleen is talking to Aiden, like in the end of the last movie. Then she walks away, and Aiden's arm bursts up through the earth." And then what, and then what, and then what? I felt like I was going to cry.

I looked down and tried to breathe deeply.

I needed a drink, I needed a drink, I needed a drink.

Well, perhaps need was the wrong word.

"Alberto's birthday was Sunday," I said. "That's when I drank. I forgot his birthday." I looked over at Sally. "I forgot. Instead of celebrating it, I got drunk and fucked Hayword and then Ryan."

OK. Technically I really hadn't been that drunk. I had been drinking.

"Oh, Mac," Sally said. "I'm so sorry."

I nodded and closed the laptop.

"Don't use Alberto as some bullshit excuse," Sally said. "You're not reading me pages because you don't have any fucking pages. Don't lie to me. Don't bullshit me. This company is my whole life."

"Really? What about your children and husband?"

"Besides them, of course, smart ass," she said, waving a hand. "No excuses. Not a single fucking one. Not Alberto's birthday. Not you fucking everyone you meet. Not drinking. I want to see the whole script by the end of the week. End of fucking story."

Sally got up.

"This visit started out so nice," I said, looking up at her.

"This is what you get for turning down my offer of sex," Sally said. She leaned down and kissed my forehead. "Now be well. No fucking around, literally. And keep in touch. Love you."

"Love you, too."

When she got to the door, she turned around and said, "Is Aiden going to live?"

I looked for something to throw at her, but everything was breakable and/or valuable.

"Leave me alone," I said.

Sally St. James left the building.

I did try to work after she left. I swear I did. But all I could see was Aiden's arm reaching out from beyond the grave, and I didn't know what to do with that. It was such a good ending. Positive, in a way. Because we left Colleen knowing that there was some hope that her son was still alive. Or alive again. So how could I follow that up? How could I end such a successful series on a high note, on a good note, making everyone happy?

I rolled my eyes. It was impossible to make everyone happy. Everyone I knew wanted Aiden to be alive somehow. Dead is dead in this world. But *Beauty and the Zombie* was about . . . zombies. It would be possible for them to come back from the dead. In fact, couldn't Colleen's true love Thomas come back from the dead? No. He had exploded with the ship.

As far as we knew.

Yes, as far as we knew.

That vodka bottle was still in my cupboard. I should throw it out. The question was: Should I drink the contents first and then throw it out? Since I hadn't had another drink in almost a day, didn't that mean I wasn't really a drunk? Maybe I could have one or two drinks now and again and all would be well. Like a normal person.

Some normal people could drink poison and survive; others couldn't.

Perhaps that was the wrong attitude: It wasn't poison. It was bliss. It was heaven. It was Nirvana in a bottle. Not the band but the state of being. Was I allowed to use that term? I wasn't Buddhist, so was it cultural appropriation? I knew a lot of Buddhists. They wouldn't give a shit if I used that word. And who I knew and what they thought was all that mattered.

I laughed. My ridiculous state of mind was apparently continuing.

Phil phoned just then.

"Hey, thanks for a nice dinner," he said. "It's the most relaxed I've been for ages. I don't know why Hayword says you're such a pain in the ass."

I laughed. I knew Hayword would never talk shit about me or his kids to anyone. "Very funny. I had a good time, too. So did you figure it out?"

"It was so easy," Phil said. "I tracked down who bought the burner phone that sent the text. I was right. It was a freelance photographer, one of the local paparazzi. Lance Johnson. You know him?"

"I don't think so," I said. "A few years ago there was a faked robbery at a restaurant where I was. After that, the outlets did stories on my rehab, showed some bad photos. But I don't know who was involved. Do you want me to go talk to him? Or do you think we should call the police?"

"If you call the police, it will get out," Phil said, "but that is what I'd advise. If he's a blackmailer, who knows what else he'd do."

"Let me think about it," I said. "Can you text me his phone and address."

Silence.

"Just for my information," I said. "I'm not going to do anything."

"I've known you a long time," he said.

"Not that long," I said. "Besides, have I ever hurt anyone?"

"Well—"

"Physically, god damnit. I've never hurt anyone physically."

"OK," he said, but he didn't sound convinced. "I'll watch him for a few days. Find out who he really is. See if there's anything we can use against him."

"That sounds good," I said. "I like that."

"By the way, Hayword called a little while ago."

"You didn't tell him about you working for me?

"Of course not," he said.

"Did he say anything to you?" I asked. "I mean, why was he calling?"

"We're friends," Phil said.

"Don't be coy," I said. "Did he tell you we'd slept together?"

"He did indeed."

Phil sounded like he was trying not to laugh. I could feel my face turning red.

"That's horrible," I said.

"He's trying to figure things out," Phil said. "He needed someone to talk with."

"I'm trying to figure things out, too," I said. "But you don't see me running around blabbing to everyone about my sex life."

"Maybe you should talk to someone," he said.

"Like you?"

"Good gawd, no," Phil said. "I don't even like you."

"I knew it!" I said. I couldn't help it: I chuckled.

"He's worried about you," Phil said. "He says you're drinking again."

I made a noise. For a little bit, Phil had been interesting. Phil had not been a part of any of the bullshit that was my life. Now . . . ugh.

"I'm not drinking," I said. "Thanks for the information, Phil. I've got to go."

"Mac, don't be like that."

I rubbed my face.

"I actually do like you," he said, rather gently. "I always have. Most people do. But you run from intimacy like a stallion running from a vet trying to geld him."

"Oh good grief," I said. "Don't pretend you're some country bumpkin."

"OK. You run from intimacy like a criminal runs from a cop," he said. "That has no punch to it."

"I've been intimate with many many people," I said. I knew what he meant, but this conversation was pissing me off.

"And I asked you to find my daughter's blackmailer," I said, "not psychoanalyze me."

"I wasn't doing that," he said.

"What did you tell Hayword?" I asked.

Phil didn't say anything for a moment. Maybe now he was pissed. "I told him people sleep with their exes all the time. It was no big deal."

I breathed a sigh of relief.

"Do you sleep with your ex all the time?"

"Are you kidding?" he said. "I've seen the dick she's sleeping with and I have no idea where his dick has been . . . so no. Besides, she humiliated me. I have no desire for her. I can barely look at her."

"I'm sorry," I said. "That must suck. Hayword has always been good to me. He's stayed a part of my life no matter what I've done."

"He's not a saint," Phil said.

"He only cheated on me once," I said, "with the blonde. And I think they only did it once."

"Yeah."

"Did you cheat on your wife?" I couldn't even remember her name. What was that about?

"No," he said. "Never did. Never had a desire to. Thought men who did that were dogs."

"How about women who did that?" I asked.

"Never had a name for them," he said. "Wasn't my business."

"I bet," I said.

We were quiet for a moment.

"You trying to be my girlfriend or something?" I asked.

"Naw, just trying to pretend to be a friend."

I laughed. "I don't have many of those. Thanks, Phil."

"Now are you gonna tell me or what?"

"Grrrr," I said. "I'll tell you the same thing I told you last night: You'll just have to wait and see when the movie comes out whether Aiden lives or dies."

"OK, OK."

"Hey, Phil, did you ever think that Aiden was like a stand-in for Alberto?"

"What? No, why? Was he?"

"I never thought about it," I said, "but one of our potential investors suggested it might be so."

"They are good entertaining movies," Phil said, "and they are layered with a whole lot of other meanings. That's what makes them feel deeper than just zombie movies. But I don't try to figure those kinds of things out. That's not the kind of mystery I try to solve."

"Huh," I said. "You are much more interesting than I would have guessed."

Phil laughed. "Most people are."

"Most people are fucking assholes," I said.

"Wow," he said. "That seems especially bitter."

I looked down at my phone as it wiggled in my hand. Hayword was calling.

"Phil, I'd love to continue this gabfest," I said, "but Hayword's calling. I'll get back with you. Thanks again. Don't forget to text me the photographer's address."

"OK. Later, Mac."

"Hi, Hayword," I said. "What's up?"

"Have you talked to Fern lately?"

"I saw her last night," I said. "Why?"

"I can't get a hold of her," he said, "and she was supposed to be at a meeting this morning. She's a no-show. That's not like her. Sally's out of the office, and I can't get a hold of anyone else who knows Fern. I'm down in Palm Springs meeting with potential investors. It would take me two hours to get back. I'm worried, Brooke. Could you go check on her?"

"I'm sure she's fine," I said. She probably was still upset about last night's meeting.

"She would have called," Hayword said. "It was a marketing meeting I asked her to go to. She wouldn't miss it."

He really gave that girl much more credit than she deserved.

"Hayword, I'm probably an hour from her apartment myself," I said. "I don't know what the traffic is doing."

"She stayed in the guest house last night," he said. "At our house."

That was a surprise.

"Was she drunk?" I asked.

"Asks the kettle about the pot. But, I don't think so. She seemed sad. I left really early so I didn't get to see her."

"OK. I'm on my way."

"I'll text her that you're coming," he said.

I grabbed my keys, put on my shoes, and was out the door. Up the winding road I went. Soon enough, I was at Hayword's house. He called it our house, but it wasn't mine, not any more. I never had any real attachment to it until we sprinkled Alberto's ashes on the backyard during an earthquake. Now I thought of it as the family home.

George, our neighborhood handyman, was climbing a tall ladder to our roof when I got out of my car.

"Watcha doing, George?" I asked as I hurried toward the door.

"Hayword asked me to put up a lightning rod because of that storm," George said.

"I thought I was the only lightning rod this family needed," I said.

George chuckled and continued up the ladder.

I used my key to the house to open the front door. As it creaked open, I heard Joanie's stiletto heels on the drive. I glanced behind me. Her car was parked at the end of the drive. She tottered toward me, waving, and clutching a huge peach-colored purse that kept dragging on the ground. She was high or drunk.

"Brooke, Brooke, I've got to talk to you," she said.

"I don't have time," I said. "I'm looking for Fern."

I went into the house. Joanie was right behind me.

"Fern!" I called. No answer.

I shut the door, walked through the house, and out the back door.

"You haven't called the police, have you?" Joanie asked. "You haven't told anyone? I was gonna go down and double-check that it was Marv's body in the car in the garage, but I got scared. I've never seen a dead body. Well, not a dead body of my husband who's been rotting there for a month."

"Joanie, shut up," I said.

I hurried across the patio and the yard to the guest house. I suddenly had a sick feeling.

I knocked on the front door.

"Fern!" I called. "Fern!"

No answer.

Joanie looked through the window.

"She's on the floor," Joanie said.

I opened the door and ran inside. Fern was on the rug next to the couch, unconscious or dead. I knelt next to her. "Fern!" I called. "Fern!"

Her lips were blue. Like Alberto's had been when he died. She seemed so small, like a child.

I felt for her pulse. If there was one, it was faint.

"What's happened?" I yelled. "Fern!" I slapped her face. "Fern!"

Nothing.

Joanie was next to me, looking around for something in her purse while she called 911. She didn't seem drunk or high any more.

"A woman is unconscious," Joanie said. "I think she's overdosed. I'm going to give her Narcan."

"What?" I said.

The whole world had slowed down. Joanie seemed to be talking very slowly.

"It won't hurt her if she's not overdosed," Joanie told me. "I take opiates sometimes, and my nurse friend got this for me." She pulled out something that looked like nasal spray. She put it up Fern's nose.

Fern gasped almost immediately. Or murmured. Something. She was alive.

"Mommy," Fern whispered.

I took my daughter in my arms and pressed her against me. *Live, live, goddamnit, live.* She felt so tiny.

"I told Jonathan," Fern whispered. "He broke up with me." She began to cry. "You were right, Mommy. I'm not good for anything."

No! I never said that. Never even thought it.

"Hang on," I said. "I'm here. Hang on."

"I saw Alberto, Mommy," she whispered. "He said to tell you hello."

"It's all right, darlin'," I said. "Everything is going to be OK."

CHAPTER NINE

I don't remember a lot about the next 24 hours. They took
Fern to the local hospital. I followed the ambulance, after grab-
bing Fern's old battered purse from the floor near her. It was one
of my old purses that I had given her years ago. Maybe even a
decade ago. She was a strange child.

I thanked Joanie for saving Fern's life.

"Remember that," Joanie said, "whenever you get the urge
to rat me out."

"Rat you out for what?" I asked her. "You haven't done anything wrong."

"Just remember that."

George was gone by the time I came out to my car again. I
glanced at the roof, but I couldn't tell if he had done anything or
not.

Hayword eventually met me at the hospital. He had to fly in
because the traffic from Palm Springs to Los Angeles to the village was so bad. I told him about the photos, the affair, and the

blackmail. When we went into Fern's cubicle, Hayword embraced her, and she sobbed while he held her. I took her hand and wouldn't let go.

I had thought she was so grown up for so long, but she was really still a girl.

"I don't know how it happened," Fern said. "I just ended up with Jonathan a few times, and he was funny. He didn't drink, so I thought that was good. But then he offered me some pills. He said he took them for his back, but they also made him high. I thought because they were prescribed it would be OK. I know, I know. I didn't realize they were opiates until I'd been doing them for a few months."

Hayword and I glanced at each other.

"I knew it was wrong to be with him," Fern said. "But he was so nice to me. He seemed to really like me. That's so alluring because no one likes me."

I wanted to say, "That's not true, Fern." But I didn't know. Maybe people didn't like her. I often didn't like her.

"That's not true, Fern," Hayword said. He gave me a look like "what the fuck?"

"People like you, Fern," I said, a little too late. "You were very popular in high school."

Fern laughed. "That was a long time ago. Besides that was because I'd give a hand job to almost anyone." Hayword groaned. Fern said, "Sorry, Dad. I don't do that any more."

No, she just ate opioids and had sex with married men. But who was I to judge?

"None of it matters," I said. "You just need to get well."

"I didn't try to kill myself," Fern said. "I took too many. If they think I tried to off myself, they'll put me in the psych ward."

"Maybe that would be a good thing," Hayword said.

"No, Daddy, please," she said. "I will go to rehab."

"I'm so sorry you are going through this," I said.

"You're not going to yell at me about bad choices?" Fern said.

I squeezed her hand. "No. You can blame me. You probably inherited my brain chemistry. There is a place in Tucson that deals with drugs and alcohol abuse as well as depression and eating disorders. Honey, you are skinny as fuck. You having trouble eating? I'm so sorry that I didn't notice. I'm so sorry I slapped you yesterday."

"What?" Hayword said. "You hit her?"

I nodded.

"I deserved it," Fern said.

"No, you didn't," I said.

"If I can get into the place in Tucson," Fern said, "I'd like to go. But what should I do about the photos? I want to tell Sally what happened. I want to apologize."

"You leave the photos to me," I said. "I will tell Sally, too, for now. You can talk to her when you're better. Right now, though, you need to get better."

After that, we all talked to doctors, and I called the rehab in Tucson and got her a place. Turned out it wasn't against the law to overdose, so we didn't have to deal with the police. Fern convinced the docs that her overdose was a mistake. I didn't know if that was true or not, but right then I went with it.

We brought Fern home that night. She slept in her old room. David sat in the chair in her room until she fell asleep. Then he came downstairs and sat with Hayword and me.

"She'll be all right," Hayword said.

"She's never been all right," David said. "Not since Alberto died. I don't think any of us have been."

"I'm sorry about that," I said. "I'm sorry that your entire childhood has been about trauma." All I seemed to be able to say was "I'm sorry."

"It's not your fault," David said. "At least not all of it."

I laughed. "Thank goodness for that."

"Can I go tomorrow when you take Fern to Tucson?" David asked. Fern said she wanted her dad to drive her. It was an eight hour drive, give or take the traffic. I offered to come, but she wanted me to be here to take care of the photos. She kept using that expression. "Take care of the photos." Like she expected me to put out a hit on the photographer or something.

Maybe that was a good idea. Every time I closed my eyes, I saw Fern lying dead on the floor of the guest house.

"You've got school," Hayword said. "I won't be back for a couple of days."

"I'll stay here with you if you like," I said.

"Yes, I would like that," David said.

"Did you tell your dad about the Whore of Hollywood list?" David's face reddened. "No."

"What?" Hayword said.

"On the dark web someone put up a list of men and said I had slept with them all. The website is called the Whore of Hollywood."

"And did you?" Hayword asked.

"No!" I said. I gave him a dirty look. How could he ask such a thing in front of our son?

"I saw the list today," I said. "I don't know who would do such a thing. Did you put it up, Hayword?"

"No!" This time he gave me a dirty look.

"I wouldn't have a clue how to do something like that," Hayword said. "And I've never seen a list."

"That's why David's been so angry with me," I said. "He's mad that I cheated on you."

Hayword nodded. "We had some bad years, your mom and I. That's all water under the bridge. We both made mistakes, but we love each other, and now we're friends." He shrugged. "It worked out."

"What do you mean you both made mistakes?" David said. "Did you cheat on Mom?"

I put a hand up. "David, our marriage is our business."

"I wish you would either be married or be divorced," David said. "It is confusing."

"It's complicated," Hayword said.

"No, it's not," David said. "That's what adults say when they don't want to do something. Climate change is complicated. No, it's not. We're burning the planet up. Whether you get a divorce or not is complicated. No, it's not. You either love each other and stay married or you don't and you get divorced."

"I don't think we're on the same scale as climate change," I said, "but I get your point. Your dad and I will talk about it."

"I've heard that before," David said.

"David, come on. I saw my daughter dead today. Can you give us a break?"

David sucked in his breath. "She was dead?"

I thought he knew that. Hayword and I looked at each other.

"The important thing is she is alive now," Hayword said.

"Is your car back from the shop?" I asked.

"Yes."

"So you can get to school tomorrow?" I said. "I might go into the office early."

"OK by me," David said.

"I'll be here when you get back from school."

David kissed us both good night, and then he went to bed. Hayword and I went up to Fern's room. She opened her eyes.

"How you feeling?" I asked.

"Like a truck hit me," she said. "I'm ready to get better."

I kissed her forehead. "Good. I might go to the office early in the morning. Do you want me to wait until you leave?"

"No," she said. "I know you've got things to take care of for me." She said it almost proudly. As though her life's goal had been achieved.

"That's right," I said.

She closed her eyes and snuggled under her covers.

"Will you say goodnight like you used to when I was little?" she asked.

I glanced up at Hayword. He shrugged.

"I'll start," Fern whispered. "See you later, alligator."

I bit my lip. "After while, crocodile."

"Take good care, grizzly bear," she said.

My lost little girl. "Bye, bye, butterfly," I said.

"Toodle loo, kangaroo," my first born murmured, a smile on her lips.

"See you soon, my raccoon," I said.

"Love you always," she whispered.

"And forever," I said.

I kissed her on the head again.

Then Hayword and I left the room. We kept her door open, but we went into our old bedroom, where Hayword slept now, and closed the door. I sat on the bed and began to cry. He put his arm across my shoulders.

"What's wrong?" Hayword asked. "Fern is OK. She's gonna be OK."

"Fern and I never said that to each other when she was a kid," I said.

"You didn't?" Hayword said. "It seemed so familiar."

"It was a scene from *Love and Other Insanities*," I said, "when the main character—Charlie—tucked her daughter in at night. Remember I named the daughter Fern, as a kind of homage to Fern, something she could see as she grew up, so she knew we loved her. Hayword, she just asked me to do something from a movie. Do you realize she is nostalgic for a mother that never existed?"

Hayword kissed the side of my face. "We all are, darlin', we all are."

Hayward and I made slow quiet love, and then we fell asleep in each other's arms. I woke up around midnight, wide awake. I slipped on my clothes and checked on the kids. Both were alive. Both slept.

I went downstairs and looked at my phone. I had several texts. Sally and Phil asked me to call in the morning. I did not look forward to talking to Sally. I also had a text from Mark. And one from Ryan.

I looked at Mark's first. "Can you come see me?" Sent hours earlier. Fuck.

I read Ryan's. "How could you do this to me?" Three hours ago. "Please come back." I stared at the phone. I thought of all those years ago when I was pregnant with Alberto. I would have done almost anything to have Ryan beg to see me. Now, I just felt numb.

I went back upstairs into Hayword's room. He was sleeping soundly. I kissed his face and put my cheek against his. He whispered in his sleep, "I love you," just like he used to do when we were together. I whispered back, "I love you, too."

Downstairs I stared out into the darkness. This was where we had spread Alberto's ashes. This was where Fern had died and come back to life this morning. This was where my family lived. It was where they belonged.

It was not where I felt I belonged.

I left the house and got in my car. Crap. Fern's purse was in my backseat. I'd never returned it. Oh well. She didn't need it now. I drove away. For a moment I thought about going to Joanie's, but she had a dead man in her garage. Didn't want to sleep there. I couldn't go to Sally's. Not until I told her what was going on between Fern and Jonathan. I got on the freeway and drove and drove.

I got off at Mark's exit. Went to his neighborhood. Drove up his drive and parked next to his truck. I sat in my car in the dark for a bit. I didn't know why I was here. Didn't know what to do. But he had asked me to come, and he had been so good to me.

I used my key to get into the house. I walked down the dark hallway to the bedroom. It no longer smelled of alcohol and urine. Or whatever it had stunk of before. I could smell Mark. I could smell his beautiful self. I took off my clothes down to my underwear. Then I got under the covers and into bed, and I spooned up behind Mark. He felt warm and familiar. I slipped my arm around him and laced it through his. He squeezed it. I breathed deeply. There. There. There. In a few moments, we were breathing together. I had loved him so much. And then, I just couldn't stand it. Love always meant loss. Always. If I kept loving him and something happened to him, where would I be?

Just as I was falling asleep, Mark turned around, and we wrapped our legs and arms around each other. "I love you," he whispered. "I know," I said. "I love you, too." *As much as I am able, I love you.* After a while, he fell asleep and then turned away from me.

I got out of bed and went to the kitchen. I opened the fridge. No booze. Opened the cupboards. No booze. Good. Good. Mark would be all right. I always knew he would be OK no matter what. Or at least that was what I used to think. Now . . . I hoped he would be all right.

I looked around. I didn't belong here either.

I took the key to his house off of my keychain, and I put it on the counter. Then I left again.

I drove to Ryan's house, which wasn't far away. I still had this gnawing in the pit of my stomach. Or ache. I got out of the car and walked up the sidewalk and rang the doorbell. Ryan opened the door almost immediately.

As soon as I stepped over the threshold, he put his arms around me. I folded myself into him, letting him envelop me.

"Thank you," he said. He no longer smelled of alcohol.

When he let me go, I said, "I'm sorry about the other day. I guess I've gone a little crazy. What can I do to help?"

He leaned down and kissed me. I gently pushed him away.

"I vomited last time we had sex," I said.

"I didn't take it personally."

"I just had sex with my husband a few hours ago," I said.

"I don't care," he said. "I can't stop thinking about you. About us."

"I think you're a complete asshole," I said.

"I am."

"Are you using?" I asked.

"Not for 24 hours," he said, "but I've got drugs and I've got alcohol. I've been staring at them. You came just in time."

"I'm not your get out of jail free fuck card," I said. "You texted me. I thought you were in trouble."

"I am."

He took my hand and led me into the kitchen. On the countertop were bottles of booze, mostly small bottles, like they have on airplanes. He had some bottles of pills and what looked to be a rock of cocaine.

"Jesus H.," I said. "What is going on here?"

"I gathered together all of the alcohol and drugs," he said. "I've been trying to decide if I should use them or not. What do you think? Do we drink and drug or throw it all out? I've been having this debate all night."

"What do you want?"

"I want to use!" he said. "But let's throw them out."

He looked at me eagerly. Please, don't let me be the cause of this, I thought.

"Let's throw them out," I said.

One by one we opened the bottles and drained them into the sink. The smell of alcohol was difficult to resist. I wanted to chug them all. Instead we rinsed each bottle out and threw them in the recycle bin. We put the pills and cocaine down the garbage disposal. I had no idea if that was all right or not. But we did it. Ryan sang and danced nearly the whole time. I was reminded of why I had fallen in love with him all those years ago: He had a happy carefree spirit. I did not. I wondered if Alberto would have been like me or Ryan?

"Anywhere else?" I asked. "Any hiding places?"

"No," he said. "This was it." He grinned. "It's all gone. I can start fresh again."

"I'm glad," I said. I wasn't sure if I was glad. I wasn't even sure why I was here. Did I belong here with this old, old lover? Someone I had loved and then loathed?

"Will you stay?" Ryan asked. "Look. I'm hard as a rock. I could go all night long."

I laughed and shook my head. "I am so glad for you."

"Glad for you, too," he said. He took me in his arms and kissed me. Part of me felt like that woman of 15 years ago who was so in love with him, and part of me felt like the me of now who didn't know him at all. I embraced him and kissed him.

"Let me tuck you into bed," I said. "And then I'm leaving."

"Awww, OK," he said.

Once we got to his bedroom, he stripped naked and then got into bed. "I am tired," he said.

I pulled the sheet and blanket up to his chin. Then I kissed him on the lips.

"Good night, Ryan," I said.

"Will I see you again?" he asked.

"I have no idea."

"Then stay."

I was tempted, but I turned off the light and left the room. I went to the kitchen to turn off the light there. I looked around. I certainly did not belong here. I reached for the light switch and spotted an unopened bottle of some kind of booze that had gotten pushed behind a roll of paper towels. I grabbed it, took off the cap, and started to pour it down the sink. Instead, I lifted it to my mouth and guzzled it.

Vodka.

I rinsed the bottle out and put it in the recycle bin. Then I left the house. I sat in the car. Fuck, fuck, fuck. I could feel the alcohol having its way with me.

I picked up my phone and called Phil. He answered sleepily.

"It's 3 a.m. and I don't do booty calls," Phil said.

"Very funny," I said. "Where do you live? Can I come over? I drank some vodka. My daughter died and came back to life today, and I drank some goddamn vodka. You're the only one at this moment that I know who I haven't fucked or fucked over. Can I sleep on your couch for a couple hours?"

"Sure, kiddo," Phil said. "I'll send you my address."

CHAPTER TEN

I woke up on Phil's couch. The clock by the front door said 11:00, and the AC was on already. It was freakin' February, and we had to use air conditioning in the morning. I threw off the blanket and sat up. I could hear Phil whistling somewhere in the near distance. Probably in the kitchen. Last night—this morning—I hadn't told Phil anything when I arrived. He had shown me the couch and handed me a pillow and a blanket. I lay down, and that was all she wrote.

Now I grabbed my phone and texted Hayword. "I couldn't sleep. I'm not drinking. Do you need me to come home?"

He immediately wrote back. "No, we've been on the road for hours. All seems well. Hey, have you seen Fern's purse?"

"No," I lied. "Maybe she left it in the Garden House. I'll check when I get back. Have a good trip."

"Love you," he said. It was automatic, something we had said to each other for decades, until we hadn't. Was love on the table now, again?

"OK," was all I managed to say. "Keep in touch." And I pressed off.

"It's slop!" Phil called.

I stood, shook myself, and walked toward the sound of his voice.

"I gotta pee first," I said as I walked into the open kitchen that had tall white cabinets, white countertops, and a black and white checked tile floor. It felt very homey.

Phil pointed, I went to the loo, and then I returned to the kitchen. He was sitting in a booth in a nook on one side of the kitchen. The windows looked out on a shady side yard. I sat in the booth across from Phil. On a peach-colored plate in front of me were two fried eggs, fried or baked breakfast potatoes, fat sausages, probably Wonder bread—toasted and buttered—and slices of peaches. I stared at the plate.

"What?" Phil asked. He was already chowing down.

"It's a little greasy," I said.

He laughed. "I ain't your chef boyfriend," he said. "Eat it or not. I don't care."

"You sound cranky," I said. I slowly put a forkful of eggs in my mouth. They were quite good.

"Yummy," I said. "Thanks for letting me stay here. You are a good girlfriend."

He shrugged. "I do my best."

I felt slightly awkward. It had been a long time since I had had a man as a friend.

"So what do we do here?" I asked. "Am I your boyfriend? Do we watch sports together? Give each other hand jobs? Bitch about women?"

Phil rolled his eyes. "You actually think men masturbate each other?" He shuddered.

"Well, Phil, some men do do that."

"I mean heterosexual men."

"I dunno. I'm not a man."

"We're human beings," he said. "Just like you."

"I doubt that."

Phil looked at me, and I grinned. "I'm just teasing you."

"You are pretty chipper for someone who said her daughter died yesterday."

"Oh yeah," I said. "I had almost forgotten about the cluster-fuck of days I've had. Our family has had. Fern overdosed. Fortunately Joanie was there with some Narcan. Saved her life."

"Joanie? Your neighbor. I think I met her a couple of times. She's cute."

"Cute?" I said. "She's a grown up ass woman. She's not cute. Although she's a lot younger than you are, so you shouldn't be lusting after her."

"I wasn't lusting," he said, "and she's not that much younger."

"I'm younger than you," I said, "and she's younger than I am. By a little."

"She looks a lot younger," Phil said.

"Because she's had a ton of plastic surgery. You could probably rip out those breasts and play ball with them."

Phil made a face. "Now why would I want to do that? See, this is why people don't like you. You always gotta argue."

"Don't say people don't like me," I said. "I might start to believe you. I could introduce you to Joanie."

"She has a husband."

Oh, fuck. I had forgotten that no one knew he was dead.

"Oh yeah," I said. "Well, she fools around a lot."

"I don't," Phil said.

"Anyway," I said. "Fern and Hayword are on the way to rehab in Tucson. I need to be home by the time David gets home from school. This whole thing has gotten him upset."

"I can imagine," Phil said. "What do you need from me?"

"Let's go confront the blackmailer," I said. "He's the reason my daughter almost died. I can't kill him—I guess. But I want him ruined."

Phil nodded. "I understand. How could you ruin him?"

"I don't know yet," I said. "You said you could go talk to him and see what his reaction is."

"Sure," Phil said, sopping up the broken yolk with his Wonder Bread and then eating it. "You can't go with me." I could barely understand what he was saying with his mouth full.

"Is this Wonder Bread?" I asked. "I haven't had Wonder Bread since I was a kid."

"No, it's just white bread," he said. "From a neighborhood baker. He has his own sourdough starter that he treats like a living thing."

"It is a living thing."

"What I'm saying," Phil said. "And he uses old flours."

"Old flours?" I said. "Heirloom? Heritage?"

"Something like that," he said. "He lets the dough rise and fall naturally. Keeps people from getting sick on bread."

"As I live and breathe," I said, "I would have never guessed you were a foodie."

"I'm not a foodie," he said. "I'm an eatie. You pay attention to the world and you know it ain't goin' so well. So I try to be responsible."

I smiled. "I love when people surprise me."

"That is so fucking condescending," Phil said.

"That's my jam," I said.

"You can't come with me," Phil repeated.

"I can come but stay in the car," I said. "I promise on my mother's grave that I won't cause any problems."

"Your mother isn't dead last I heard."

I shrugged. "She will be someday."

"We'll all be dead one day," he said. "So swear on your own grave."

"No! That's just asking for trouble. My mother can take care of herself."

"All right," he said. "The blackmailer doesn't live far from here. You keep down, and you keep shut up."

I rolled my eyes. "OK, boss."

We ate the rest of our meal in silence. When we were finished, I said, "That was really good. I almost feel normal."

"And what is normal to you?" Phil asked.

I thought for a moment. "I don't know. Normal seems to be that I'm always on the verge of disaster. Trauma is around every corner."

"You sound like a lot of cops," Phil said. "They get so used to trauma that it feels better when they're in the midst of some kind of shit storm. They're always fucking up in their lives—because disaster feels normal. Fortunately, I am not that way. I'm glad to be retired. I don't need the trauma or the drama."

"No," I said. "That's not right. I like peace and quiet."

Although I did get nervous when everything in my life calmed down. Didn't everyone? Because it couldn't last, the good times, right? Something bad was always around the corner.

I said, "I'm not like those cops. I want everything to settle down. It just never does."

"I hear ya," Phil said. "But I've never known you when things were settled down."

"Are you saying I cause all these things that happen in my life, like my kid dying?"

"Jesus, no," Phil said. "We all have real things happen in our lives, horrible things." Phil gulped the last of his coffee and then he said, "So, you ready to go find this dirt bag?"

We took Phil's car. The dirt bag lived in a house on the edge of a nice part of the city.

"I guess blackmail pays well but not that well," I said when Phil pointed out the house. We parked down the road a bit.

"Stay low," Phil said.

"What are you going to say?"

Phil shrugged. "I'll wing it. People talk to me."

That didn't sound like much of a plan. I picked up my phone and called Phil. He answered it. "Yes?"

"Keep it on," I said. "I want to listen to it all."

Phil made a face, but he put the phone in his pocket. "Whatever you hear, you stay the fuck in this car."

"Yes, grandpa," I said.

Then he got out of the car and began walking down the street.

"Can you hear me?" he asked.

It was muffled, but I could hear him.

"Yep," I said.

"Don't talk," he said.

"Yeah, right," I said.

I watched him walk up to the house. Heard the doorbell ring from his phone.

Door squeaking open. Children's voices in the background laughing. Then a man's voice. "May I help you?"

"Are you Lance Johnson?" Phil.

"Yes." He hesitated.

"I am Phil Case," Phil said. "I'm a private investigator. May I speak with you in private?"

"We're just about to get ready to go to church," Johnson said. I could see a man stepping outside. Closing the door. He was probably in his forties, red hair, a complexion that was not suited for Los Angeles.

"What is this about?" Johnson asked.

Phil had stepped back a bit. Must be his training as a police officer.

"You've been blackmailing a client of mine," Phil said, "and I wanted to talk to you about it before we report it to the police."

"Which client?" the man asked.

I covered my mouth so I wouldn't gasp. He was doing this to more than one person?

"How many people are you blackmailing?" Phil asked.

"I wouldn't call it blackmail," Johnson said.

This guy was a talker. Good.

"I offer people a chance to buy back photos they don't want made public."

"Photos you've taken," Phil said.

"Most of the time," he said, "but not always. They all know that if they go to the police, I will hand over the photos to the tabloids. That's our deal."

"Deal?" Phil said. "I don't think any of them willingly made a deal with you."

Johnson laughed. "You'd be surprised. I have one girl who gave me the address of what hotel she'd be at so I could take photos of her and her married lover. Then she asked me to pretend to blackmail her, and we could split the money. She said 80/20. I said 50/50. She works for a studio, but she has a drug problem."

I was getting sick to my stomach. Obviously he was talking about Fern.

"The joke's on her, though," Johnson said, "because I've got the photos and I will release them if she doesn't come up with the money."

"You seem pretty proud of yourself," Phil said.

"A guy's got to make a living," Johnson said. "I've got two daughters and a wife. None of them contribute a dime. But praise Jesus, they are all good girls."

"Phil," I whispered to myself. "Ask him who the woman is, ask him who the woman is."

"So if someone named Fern Lightman asked you to track me down," Johnson said "tell her she still has a few days to get me the money. Otherwise, I'm sending those photos everywhere. The photos of her mother, too. I'm sending them everywhere, too."

"Photos of her mother?"

"Yeah, that writer. Brooke McMurphy. It's all legal. Fern let me in so I could install cameras in McMurphy's house and car. Fern said she was part owner of everything so it was OK." Johnson laughed. "I tell you one thing: She is not a very good daughter. Can you imagine doing that to your mother?"

"Did you give her the photos you took of her mother?"

"No, not yet," Johnson said. "I haven't seen her yet. I'm meeting her at my office at 4 p.m. Bad traffic time, but I'll get something more out of it. She's a great roll in the hay despite everything. She's meaner than hell. If my wife ever found out, I'd be done for. But you gotta do what you gotta do. Good talking with you, man. Just tell whoever it is to buy the photos from me, and then we're all good."

And then Johnson went back into the house.

It took everything in my power not to jump out of the car and run after him. To kill him. Or at least slay him with my wit.

As Phil walked back to the car, he took out his phone and hung up on me. A few moments later, he got into the car.

He looked at me. "I-I don't know what to say, Brooke. I'm speechless."

"What a fucking piece of shit," I said.

"Who? Him or your daughter."

I stared at him. "Both."

CHAPTER ELEVEN

I was so angry I was speechless. No, that's the wrong word. I was enraged. I saw red. No, I saw scarlet. That's how pissed I was. I wanted to call Hayword and tell him to drop Fern off at the side of the road. But no, no, I couldn't do anything yet. I had to think, think.

Phil tried to talk to me, but it was as if I couldn't hear anything except the voices in my own head. How could Fern do this to me, her own mother? Every time I thought we had come to some kind of understanding, she would do something to blow it all up. She burned down our house—or she didn't. The jury was out on that now as far as I was concerned. She staged a robbery in the restaurant where we were having breakfast to get her then-boyfriend a job. And now . . . this. What was *this?* Was she trying to get revenge on me for something or just make a boatload of money?

"She's an addict," I heard Phil say. "Her brain isn't right."

I looked over at him. It seemed like he was in the passenger's seat, and I was in the driver's seat.

"You should understand that," Phil said.

No, Phil was driving. Thank god.

"Why should I understand that?" I asked. "Because I'm a drunk? I never hurt anyone except myself."

Phil made a noise and shook his head.

"What?" I said. "And be careful with your answer because I want to punch someone, and you're the only one near."

"Like you scare me," he said. "You hurt everyone around you. Your husband especially. Your kids."

"But never on purpose," I said. "I didn't have a plan. It just happened."

"And Fern's worse because she had a goddamn plan?"

"Fuck, yes," I said.

"What are you gonna do?" he asked.

"You mean after I kill her?" I said. "I'm gonna bury her body where no one will ever find it."

When we got back to Phil's house, I felt a bit more grounded. My anger had dulled enough for my feelings to be hurt, for a moment, and then I was angry again.

Phil got into my car and dug around until he found a tiny camera where one of the plug-ins was.

"The photos were automatically sent to the satellite and then probably to Johnson's computer," Phil said, pointing to something on the camera. "But there's also a memory card, for extra protection in case anything went wrong."

"But we know he got photos," I said, "because he mentioned them. Nothing went wrong from his point of view."

Phil pulled out the memory card and handed it to me.

"What am I gonna do with this?" I asked.

"You can see what he has if you like," Phil said. "I can put the memory card in my camera and then download it onto my computer."

"I don't want you to see these," I said.

"OK, then *you* can put them in my camera and download them onto my computer. You know what a computer is, right? And you know what downloading is?"

"Shut up," I said. I snatched the memory card from him. We closed the door to the car and walked toward Phil's front door. "Although really, I don't know the difference between uploading and downloading. You?"

"Absolutely no clue," Phil said.

Phil put the card into his camera and showed me how to download the photos onto his computer, without him looking at them. Then he left his office and closed the door behind him as one after another of the photos came up in a line on the screen.

Ryan and I sitting together in the car. Looks like we are talking. I hold up the vodka-laced OJ jug. He drinks. I pull off my slacks. Good god. Close up of my bare ass. They say the camera adds twenty pounds. This camera added a hundred pounds. My ass was too close to the camera. Oh fuck. Ryan's erection. Me putting a condom on his dick. Me sitting on his penis. Nothing sexy about it. And no mistaking who we were.

If these photos were published, my family would be destroyed. For my children to know I was fucking Ryan hours after I had slept with their father. Gawd.

Not that I cared about what Fern thought at this moment, but there was David to consider. And Hayword. The media would dig up the story of Alberto, his death, our house burning down, me later going into rehab. I did not want to relive that courtesy of the 'bloids.

Plus, this would not be good for Ryan. Especially if someone figured out he was an alcoholic, and the OJ was really a screwdriver. He would look like a victim, and I would look like . . . what I was. An enabler. Or worse.

Jesus.

Fuck, fuck, fuck.

I could see it now in the tabloids: First photos of Hayword and I doing it with the timestamp plain and visible while our private parts would be covered with a black line? Then photos of me and Ryan, only hours later.

I deleted the photos from Phil's computer and took the memory card from his camera and slipped it into my front shirt pocket.

I went into the living room where Phil sat with his feet up on the coffee table. He looked up at me.

"That bad?" he asked.

"You have no idea," I said as I sat in the chair opposite him. "I was having sex with an old love hours after having sex with Hayword."

There, I had said it out loud.

"That's what Johnson has photos of?" Phil asked.

"Yes," I said. "It's not a good way to figure out I need to lose about 30 pounds either."

Phil laughed. I guess it would be funny if it were happening to someone else.

"What about the camera in the house?" Phil asked.

"It'll show Hayward and I having sex, I assume," I said.

"You think it would hurt Hayword if those photos were published of you and this other man?" Phil asked. "Even though you're separated. I don't think it would be a big deal."

"It would be to my family," I said. "The other man was Alberto's father, the one who deserted me when I got pregnant all those years ago."

"Jesus," Phil said. "How did you happen to get together with him again?"

I groaned. "It's too sordid to talk about."

"Remember I was a police officer," he said.

"I went crazy a couple days ago. That's all. And right now I need to remove that camera from my bedroom and then figure out what to do next."

Lance Johnson thought he was meeting Fern at 4:00 today at his office. I looked at the clock. I needed to delay that meeting until I figured out what I was doing.

"Phil, can you tell me where to look for the camera in my house?" I asked.

"I'll find it for you," he said.

"You are being so nice. Don't you have some work to do?"

He laughed. "This is work," he said. "I'm charging you for every minute."

"OK then," I said. "I'll meet you at my bungalow around 2:30. I'll text you the address."

He nodded. "I expect food!" he called after me as I headed for the door.

"I don't do booty calls," I said.

I heard his chuckle as I headed out the door.

I hurried to my car and texted Phil the address. Then I dug Fern's phone out of her purse. I looked through her contacts. There was Lance Johnson's name, plain as day. I texted him from Fern's phone, "Got tied up today. Can I meet you tomorrow morning at your place? I'll have the money."

I held my breath, hoping that Fern had not gotten a hold of him some other way. I stared at the screen.

"Come on, you dirt bag," I said.

"10 a.m. Be there or don't you dare," he wrote.

I texted a thumbs up emoji.

"Phew." I now had a few hours to figure this out.

I texted Sally, "I need to see you. Where are you?"

"My house," she texted right back.

I put her address in my GPS. Shouldn't take too long. No major traffic jams.

"Can I come over? We need to talk."

I was already on my way. I heard the phone beep with her reply, but I didn't look. I didn't want to be discouraged. This was going to be a terrible conversation that could ruin our friendship as well as our business.

I had to do it. I couldn't go forward until I knew what Sally wanted and how she would react.

I was almost there when the phone rang. My car answered it.

"You driving?" Hayword asked.

"Hands-free," I said, "remember, you made sure my car had it. Are you in Tucson?"

He hesitated. Then he said, "Not yet. Fern wanted to stop at Quartzsite to look for some rocks. We kind of lost each other."

"She's probably off buying drugs," I said.

"No," Hayword said. "She's been so loving and sincere."

Just like last night when she was so loving toward me. Fake, fake, fucking fake.

"We're supposed to meet at this little café," Hayword said. "It'll be all right."

"A little café in Quartzsite?" I said. "That sounds doubtful. Be careful, Hayword; all is not what it seems."

"What do you mean?" he asked.

"I'll talk to you about it later," I said, "when I know more."

"OK," he said. "I love you."

"Why are you saying that now?" I asked.

"Because I do," he said.

"Look, we had sex a couple of times," I said. "It was nice. But we're not getting back together or anything."

"Our daughter died yesterday," he said. "I figure I want everyone in my life to know when I love them. And I fucking love you. Even though you are such a pain in the ass. Maybe because you are a pain in the ass."

"Fuck you," I said. "I fucking love you, too, but it doesn't mean anything, except that I love you and I'd protect you with my last breath."

"Yeah, me, too," he said. "Call me."

He was right: Fern had almost died yesterday. She hadn't faked that. Joanie had given her the Narcan. The paramedics had taken her away.

I squinted. Only the doctors never told us anything specific. Because she wasn't a minor. Her records were private.

Could she have faked her overdose and her death?

Fuck. Could that be true? What was real? How could she have pretended to die in front of me, after I had already lost one child?

I turned into Sally's long paved drive. It wound up and around a hill. True Beverly Hills style. Her place made ours look like a log cabin. I parked the car and walked up the palatial steps to her huge wooden front door. I rang the bell. A tall thin white woman dressed all in black opened the door. Was she the maid, the housekeeper, Sally's new love interest?

"May I help you?"

"Sally's expecting me," I said. "I'm Brooke McMurphy."

"Ah yes," the woman said. "Come in."

I stepped over the threshold, and she closed the door behind me. She led the way across Sally's huge living room and down several steps toward the patio.

"I love the zombie movies," the woman said solemnly.

I wished people would stop calling them that.

"Can you tell me if Colleen's son Aiden will come back to life in the third movie?" she asked.

I almost burst out laughing as I followed her. She didn't even turn around and look at me as she asked the question.

"I guess we'll have to wait and see," I said as I followed her outside.

She pointed to Sally who was sitting by the pool under an umbrella.

"Dead or alive," the woman said as she walked by me. "I'd fuck him."

I stood with my mouth open for a moment as she went back into the house.

"What the fuck?" I whispered. Then I walked down the steps and across the grass to the pool where Sally lounged. She was wearing a one piece black bathing suit that made her white skin look even whiter. She tilted her head and her black hat up when she saw me. She smiled, but her eyes looked dead. Uh-oh.

"Lovely to see you so soon again," she said. "Why aren't you working?"

"Why aren't you?" I asked. I sat in the chaise lounge next to her. I felt entirely overdressed.

"I can have Maude get you a bathing suit," Sally said.

"So that's Maude," I said. "Is she new?"

"New to this world or new to us?"

"Either or both."

Sally laughed. "Yes and no."

Didn't matter.

"I need to talk to you about some things," I said. "I don't know where to begin."

"I know you fucked Hayword and Ryan," she said. "And you forgot your dead kid's birthday. Again." She was flipping through a magazine like this was nothing.

"His name is Alberto," I said.

Sally looked over at me. "What?"

"My dead kid's name."

She blinked. "OK. You forgot Alberto's birthday. Again."

"What the fuck, Sally?"

She threw the magazine down. "If you're trying to tell me that your whore of a daughter fucked my husband and someone took photos of it and they're blackmailing your daughter with them, I already know." She was trembling. "Jonathan told me this morning. You should have told me."

"I just found out," I said.

"When?"

"When?"

"Yes, when did you fucking find out?"

"I-I think it was Monday," I said.

"And here it is already Wednesday," Sally said. "How could you not tell me?"

Wednesday. Wasn't that the day of David's lightning storm? I looked up at the sky. Blue, blue, blue.

"I was trying to figure everything out," I said.

"Figure out what?" Sally said. "How you could get away with it? How you could get your daughter off the hook?"

"How not to hurt you," I said. "How not to destroy our friendship. Fern overdosed yesterday and died. Apparently she was distraught because Jonathan broke up with her when he found out about the blackmail, Monday night. Joanie gave her Narcan. She's on the way to rehab today. I hired Phil Case to find out who was doing the blackmailing. It's a pap, Lance Johnson. But he said Fern hired him."

Sally drew in her breath. "What?"

"That's all I know right now," I said. "I wanted to let you know. I'm going to Fern's apartment right now. I haven't spoken to her since I found out she had something to do with it. Apparently she's a drug addict, and she needs money. I guess. I don't really know."

Sally picked up her phone and shouted into it, "Get my asshole of a husband out here."

A few moments later, Jonathan stepped out of the house and

walked toward us. He looked smaller. Or something. Much diminished since last I saw him in real life. Strange not to see my daughter naked on top of him.

"Hello, Brooke," he said.

Sally waved to him, as if to keep him from getting any closer.

"When did you break it off with the whore Fern?" Sally asked.

"Hey," I said. "Just call her Fern. A woman calling another woman a whore diminishes us all."

Sally gave me a look—I can't describe it more than to say it was as if we were complete strangers and she hated me thoroughly.

"When did you break it off with the cunt slut Fern?" Sally asked.

Jonathan looked from Sally to me and then back again. "As I told you, she broke it off from me. She told me a month ago that she was being blackmailed with photos of us, and she needed a million dollars. When I told her I didn't have it, she broke it off. Not right away but soon after."

"She didn't realize that Jonathan hasn't worked for a while and that I've been supporting his ass," Sally said. "He told me about it last night because Fern told him the photos would be published unless I could give her money to give to the blackmailer. Jonathan doesn't care about the photos, and neither do I. What do I care if Fern's reputation is in pieces?" She shrugged.

Sally waved Jonathan away. He turned and left. I had more questions, but apparently she was done with him.

Sally found a cigarette somewhere and lit it.

"I thought there was something in your prenup about not smoking," I said.

"There's also something about him not fucking someone

young enough to be his daughter. Almost young enough." She took a long drag on the cigarette.

"I'm so sorry about this, Sally."

She looked at me. "You should be. It's all your fault. Fern despises you. She blames you for everything. Couldn't you see that?"

"I thought that had all gotten better," I said.

"And these movies are paeans to your dead son," Sally said. "Fern has no place in your life. So she emulates you. Fucking everyone and drinking like a fish."

"I never slept with married men," I said. "Or women."

"Oh, who gives a fuck?" Sally said.

"Where do we go from here?" I asked.

"Fern is fired," Sally said.

"Of course," I said.

"And you better have the script finished to show the investors on Monday," she said, "or our contract will be null and void, you will no longer be a part of Back to Life Studios, and all the profits from the first two movies go to me. And Hayword. Once I tell him you fucked Ryan, he won't be very sympathetic toward you. So you will have nothing."

She smashed out her cigarette on the side of her chair.

"Any questions?" she asked.

"Wow," I said, "it's as if you were waiting for this to happen."

She smiled. "I was. I knew you'd fuck it up eventually. That's who you are. Like daughter, like mother."

I got up to leave.

"I'm sorry I ever fucked you," I said. "I never knew you were such a dick."

CHAPTER TWELVE

I felt dazed as I drove toward home. Couldn't tell you how I got there. I wanted to call someone. But who? Mark. Mark was supposed to be my true love, but that had gone awry. I couldn't tell Hayword, not yet. I couldn't deal with him falling apart as our life was falling apart. Joanie had enough on her plate.

Clearly I needed more friends.

Sally was right about the contract. I had to perform or I was done. I had agreed to it because I couldn't imagine that I wouldn't perform. It just wasn't in my nature to miss a deadline.

I needed help.

Joanie had said magic was possible if a lightning storm was coming. "I see no sign of a lightning storm," I said, "but Nature gods, can you help me get out of this, keep my children safe, and help us live happily ever after?"

Phil drove up almost at the same moment as I drove up the drive to my bungalow.

"How'd it go with Sally?" Phil asked.

"Not good," I said.

I let Phil into the house. He looked around. "I've heard about this place for years. I figured it would be fancier."

I rolled my eyes as I shut the door. "What on earth could you have heard about this house?" Phil looked at me. "Never mind. I don't want to know."

I showed Phil to the bedroom. It didn't take him long to find the camera. This one I was able to hook right up to my computer. There we were, Hayword and I fucking our brains out. Not attractive at all. If this was what porn looked like, how did anyone ever get turned on?

I went out to my living room where Phil waited for me. We sat in silence for a bit.

"I looked around the rest of the house," he said. "I didn't find any other camera. When do you think they put the cameras in?"

I had no idea. Wait.

"Fern stopped by Friday night," I said. "She left me a note and a present. Martinelli's cider and cherry pie. I wonder if that's when they did it. She would have known I was away because we were at David's school."

It was the next day that I had started to feel stressed out, or something.

When the next day?

In the afternoon.

What had happened?

I had eaten the pie and drank the Martinelli's Fern had left.

I suddenly felt sick to my stomach.

I got up and went to the fridge, opened it, and took out the bottle of Martinelli's. Just a swallow or two remained in the bottom of it. I got a glass from the open shelves and poured a bit of the cider into it. Then I brought it to Phil. He took a sip.

"What is it?" I asked.

"It's apple cider," he said, "and champagne."

I almost fell to my knees. I staggered to the couch. Could this be true: My own daughter had spiked my cider. She had wanted me to drink again. Why?

What would happen if I became a sloppy drunk again?

Fern knew if I began drinking again I would do something embarrassing. Then she would have the photos from the camera they installed in my car and my bedroom. Or the blackmailer would have photos.

Fern was the reason everything fell apart on Sunday. She was the reason I drank on Sunday.

She did all of this to get money? Why hadn't she just asked me for money? Why hadn't she told me she was in trouble? Was it easier to ruin my life than to ask for money? Or was ruining my life the reason for it all?

My own daughter had spiked my drink.

How could she?

How could I have handed Ryan a jug of spiked OJ.

Almost handed it to him.

I had told him. At least I had told him. I didn't just give it to him to drink without him knowing.

How had Hayword and I raised such a monster?

"What am I missing?" Phil asked.

"Fern brought me this sparkling apple cider," I said. "She left it in my kitchen. It was open. I just thought she'd taken a sip before leaving it, but she had opened it so she could put alcohol in it. When I drank it on Saturday, I was tired, cranky. I didn't notice it had alcohol in it. Fern is the reason I started drinking on Sunday. She's the reason this blackmailer now has photos of me with Hayword and me with Ryan."

"Jesus," Phil said.

"Understatement," I said. I took a deep breath. "I've got to get home to David and then call Hayword and tell him."

"Is there anything else I can do for you?" Phil asked.

"Text me Johnson's office address," I said. "I might need to have a conversation with him."

"Don't go see him alone," Phil said. "He might be dangerous."

"So am I," I said.

We looked at each other. Finally he shrugged. "OK. But at least call me and tell me what you're doing."

"I will definitely try to do that," I said. "Thank you for everything. Hey, could you call Caryn at our offices? She was trying to figure out who put that list up of all the men I'd slept with. Maybe you could help her. I want it taken down. It's causing David some stress."

Phil nodded. "Will do. I think I might go see my kids tonight."

I laughed or moaned. "Make sure none of them are psychopaths."

"Fern isn't a psychopath," Phil said.

"Really?" I said. "Then what?"

"I don't have an answer to that," he said. "I'll talk to you tomorrow."

I followed him out the door. We said goodbye, and I drove up to my old house. David was inside, already home from school.

"Hello, darlin'," I said. "I thought you weren't getting home until later today." He looked distressed. "What's going on?"

"I got the mail for the Alberto Foundation," he said. "The bank statements. There are two checks written out to people I don't know. I called the bank, and they say they've got my signature on them, along with Fern's. Because there has to be two signatures, remember. The four of us, and there has to be two. But I don't know these people. They have to be organizations doing work on climate change because that's our mission. Mom, the checks are for $50,000 each."

"Oh, shit," I said. He held out the bank statement to me, and I looked at it. Yep, two checks, on the same day.

"Who were they made out to?" I asked.

He looked down at a piece of paper where he had written the names. "Sue Smith and Connie Kelly."

"Fuck," I said. Clearly made-up names.

Obviously Fern had stolen the money.

"We're a non-profit," David said. "This is against the law. I could go to jail."

"No, David, listen, you are not going to jail. I will fix this. Try to calm down. Um, get yourself a snack. I'm going to call our accountant."

I ran up to Hayword's office, sat in his chair, and then called our accountant, Marjorie Banks. We greeted each other, and then I said, "We found out that two unauthorized checks were written on the Foundation account for $50,000 each. We believe it was Fern and she forged her brother's signature. She has a drug problem. She's on her way to rehab. What can we do to make certain David isn't in trouble and that we aren't in trouble?"

"First, you need to put the $100,000 back," Marjorie said. "I can do that for you if you like. Transfer it from your savings account and put it in the Foundation's account. We need to get Fern off of everything to do with the Foundation. I'll do what I can do, but you need to talk to your lawyer, too, to see who you need to report it to."

"OK," I said. "Thanks, Marjorie."

Then I phoned Hayword. I took a deep breath. He answered.

"Hi, Brooke," Hayword said. "I've got her. She's fine. No drugs. We're in a hotel for the night."

"I've got a lot to tell you, Hayword," I said. "Fern hired the blackmailer. I don't know all the details. We'll have to ask her. She was trying to get us or Sally to pay the blackmail."

"What?"

"Yes," I said. "Phil talked to the photographer today. They also put a camera in my car and my bedroom in the hopes of being able to blackmail me. They did it Friday night."

Hayword made a noise. "What the fuck? But-but, there will be photos of us having sex. They can't blackmail us about that. We're married."

"When they put in the cameras, they left a bottle of Martinelli's apple cider and pie," I said.

"I remember you told me about that," Hayword said.

"There was alcohol in the cider," I said. "That's the reason I drank Sunday—because I had already been drunk Saturday."

"What the fuck? Why would she do that?"

"You'll have to ask her," I said. "There's more. She stole $100,000 from the Foundation. I think she may be going to jail. I called Marjorie and told her to put the money back, but I don't know if that'll make a difference."

"Fuck," Hayword said. "I think I should bring her home then, instead of rehab. We've got to figure this all out."

"Oh, Hayword," I said, "it is so fucked up. That's not even all of it." I felt like I was going to cry. "I can't tell you over the phone. Please just come home. I don't care what you do with her. Leave her at rehab. Leave her at the side of the road. I don't care."

"She's still our daughter," Hayword said.

"Who gave an alcoholic a drink," I said. "I had no fucking idea. It was apple cider. I just thought it was was cider, Hayword." I began to weep. "I had no idea. The things I did. They were awful."

"Having sex with me wasn't that awful," he said quietly.

I laughed through my tears.

"It will be OK," Hayword said. "We'll get through this."

"Sally says if I don't get the script finished, I'm done. All the profits from the first two movies will go to her and to you and I'll be out."

"Then we have to make the time and space for you to do the script," Hayword said. "If that's what you want."

"But you have no idea what I've done," I said, "since Sunday. You have no idea. You will never love me again. It will never be right. She has ruined us all."

"I'll be home tomorrow," Hayword said. "We'll fix this then. Brooke, there's nothing you could do that would make me stop loving you. Haven't you figured that out yet? It will be OK."

"I don't think it will be," I said, "but thanks for saying it. I need to go calm David down. Fern forged his signature on the checks. He's afraid he's going to jail."

"Jesus," Hayword said. "I'll talk with you tonight."

I hurried back downstairs. David was at the kitchen island, shaking. I put my arms around him.

"It's OK, sweetheart," I said. "You are not in trouble. The money is being put back even as we speak."

"Who were those people?" David said. "Who did she give all that money to?"

"My guess is that she gave it to herself," I said.

"You mean those were pseudonyms?"

"Something like that," I said. "Did you know she was using drugs?"

David shook his head. "No. Something was up. She was always mad when I talked to her."

"Really? As far as I can remember, she's always been mad." I shouldn't have said it, but I was tired of it.

"She kept talking about not having money," David said, "and how we deserved more because of how we grew up."

"Is that how you feel?" I asked. "Do you think I should pay you because you had a shitty childhood?"

David looked at me. He wasn't shaking any more. He suddenly looked like an adult. He was so handsome: a cross between me and Hayword.

"I didn't have a shitty childhood," he said. "My brother died. My mother has a chronic illness. Those are the bad things. I have parents who love me and take care of me. I live in a nice house. I always have food and shelter. That doesn't sound shitty to me."

I put my arms around him, and we embraced.

"Then why have you been acting so crappy lately?" I asked as we let each other go.

He shrugged. "Come on, Mom. You explained this to me when I was 13 years old. I've got a lot of hormones cascading through my body and my body is often ahead of my brain. It makes me fucking cranky."

"Goddamn it," I said. "You're not supposed to be swearing." I smiled.

"And I didn't like seeing that list," David said.

"But it's not true or real," I said.

"I know that now."

"I guess your electrical storm never happened," I said. "That's good news."

"Mom, do you ever look at the news? Massive thunderstorms are supposed to hit the LA area Thursday along with the lightning storm."

"I have been a little preoccupied this week," I said.

"I gotta tell you something."

Oh shit. Was he on drugs? Had he knocked someone up? Stolen something? Was he quitting school?

"Aunt Joanie called me over to look at something in her back garage."

My stomach lurched.

"She's not your aunt," I said. "I don't know why you call her that."

Yep. That's what I said. Good grief.

"So what did you find?"

"I went down there," David said, "but it smelled like something died. It was horrible. I almost threw up. I opened the side garage door and it looks like there's someone in the front seat of the Jaguar. You know, dead."

"Did you get close?"

"No," he said. "I ran like hell. Aunt Joanie told me she thought Uncle Marv was dead in the Jaguar. She called him that. I've never called him Uncle Marv. I think I've met him twice. Joanie said she didn't want to call the police unless someone was really there. She thinks he's haunting her."

"Oh Jesus H. Christ," I said. "I cannot believe she got you in the middle of this."

"Do you think she killed Marv, and she was trying to get me to take the fall for it?"

"No. She knows if she hurt you in any way I would beat her to a pulp."

David laughed.

"What?" I said.

"Come on, Mom," he said. "You're this tiny thing. You ain't gonna beat anyone up."

"You know nothing," I said. "I'm a tough old broad."

"I don't doubt that," he said. "You know, old and tough."

I slugged his arm. "Oh, aren't you funny. I'm gonna go talk to your aunt."

"Can I come?" he asked.

"Um, there might be some swearing," I said. "I won't be long."

I left the house, walked across the street and down some until I came to Joanie's driveway. I walked into the house without knocking. Joanie was sitting on the couch, as usual, sipping a drink, as usual.

"What the fuck, Joanie?" I said.

She looked surprised to see me and then terrified.

"I didn't know she was really going to overdose," Joanie said. "It was supposed to be a joke. Let's scare Brooke, you know, ha ha."

"What? What the fuck are you talking about?"

Joanie closed her mouth.

"What are you talking about?" she asked.

"Oh my gawd," I said. "So it was all a put on. Fern didn't really overdose? She asked you to come over and give her Narcan so I would think she had died?"

Joanie put her drink down. "A joke. A fucking joke. She said the two of you had been playing practical jokes on one another lately. This was just another one."

"But you called the ambulance. You really gave her the Narcan. Didn't you?"

"Because she was blue," Joanie said. "I figured that's what I should do. She was supposed to open her eyes and wink at me or something. But she was fucking dead."

"What is wrong with you, Joanie?" I said. "I found my baby boy dead. What kind of person would think it was a funny practical joke if I found my daughter dead? I mean what the holy fuck were you thinking? Didn't that seem like a screwy thought process?"

"I don't know!" Joanie said. "Fern has always been weird, and she was talking about what a stick-in-the-mud you were now, and wouldn't it be funny if you thought she overdosed. Of course now that I say it out loud it sounds terrible. But I was drunk, and my husband is out there rotting in the garage and haunting me. He's fucking haunting me. I hear all kinds of noises in the night now, Brooke."

"That's another thing," I said. "David said you asked him to go check and see if there was a dead man in the Jaguar. Don't involve my kids in your bullshit. Go down there yourself. Or call the police."

"OK, OK. I just didn't know who to call."

"So you called my son?" I looked at her. "You haven't done anything inappropriate with him, have you?"

"What?" she asked. "No. What do you mean inappropriate?"

"Have you had sex with him?" I asked. "Have you given him anything to drink? Given him drugs."

"Christ," Joanie said. "No! He's like a son to me."

"Fuck you," I said. "You have no idea what that even means. I don't want any thing more to do with you, Joanie. This is it. If you contact us again, I'll call the police and tell them you have a dead man in your garage."

"I know all your secrets," Joanie said. "The things I could tell."

I laughed. "Wow. That didn't take you long. You actually don't know any of my secrets." I turned around to leave.

"What about Marv haunting me?" she asked.

"Marv is not haunting you," I said.

"How do you know?"

"Because there are no such things as ghosts," I said. "My guess is that you're overly sensitive because you're letting your husband rot in the fucking garage. If you really think you're hearing things, maybe Marv is gaslighting you. Maybe he's got a girlfriend and the two of them are trying to drive you crazy. Get some nanny cams and put them up around the house. If someone is really doing something you'll catch them."

"That's brilliant," Joanie said. "Thank you! Are you really not my friend any more?"

"Joanie, you let me believe my daughter was dead."

"But she was dead."

"But you thought she wasn't and you thought it would be a

fun prank. This is hurting my brain. I am leaving. Your problems are your own now."

"What if someone killed Marv? They could be roaming our neighborhood looking for other victims."

"Call the fucking police," I said as I went out the door.

"Christ," I said to myself as I crossed the road. Two of my best women friends gone in a day. I didn't care. Everyone needed a friend, sure, but I did not need another problem.

I hurried home. So friendless I would be.

CHAPTER THIRTEEN

David and I stir-fried chicken, along with broccoli and carrots we cut into matchsticks. He told me about his day in school. He smiled and laughed. I listened. We sat at the counter and ate together. I liked hearing about his friends. For a long while, Hayword and I had been worried that he didn't have any. His friends now seemed so engaged in the world. David, too. I hoped it wasn't all too much for them. I didn't hang onto that thought. I loved being with my son. It was just the two of us. I was OK with that. I didn't think about Alberto not being there, or about Fern being a drug addict. It was just me and my boy.

When we had almost finished eating, David said, "You drank on Sunday, didn't you? I'm not mad at you. I just want to know."

"I did," I said.

"Do you know why?"

I sighed. I didn't know how much I should tell him.

"The real reason is that I'm a drunk," I said, "and drunks drink."

"But you didn't for so long," he said.

I nodded. "That's true. And I didn't feel like I was about to relapse. But I wasn't truthful about my relationship with Mark. I couldn't be real and truthful with him."

"Mom," David said, "I don't like secrets."

I pressed my lips together. "Fern gifted me a bottle of sparkling cider," I said. "I drank it. Turns out, it was spiked with champagne. I didn't notice." I shrugged. "I feel really stupid. I should have known."

"That's terrible, Mom," David said. "How could she do that? I don't ever want to see her again. And to think we were so worried about her when she overdosed. I don't get it. Why would she want you to relapse?"

"I don't really know," I said. "I think she thinks she needs money and figured she could get it from me if I was drunk." He didn't need to know about the cameras or the blackmail. That information was too much for me, and I was an adult. I wasn't going to burden him with it. Not yet.

"What are you going to do?" David asked.

"Your dad and I will talk later," I said. "We'll figure out something."

"Will she go to jail for stealing from the Foundation?"

"Probably," I said.

"Good. I hope she rots there. I hope she gets some kind of STD and actually rots there."

"That's pretty specific," I said. I put my arm across his shoulders. "I am so angry with your sister. More angry than I have ever been with anyone. And I know that she's obviously got some problems."

"Do you think she's a psychopath?" David asked. "Do you think she's gonna kill us all in our sleep?"

There went his anxiety.

"I don't think she's a psychopath," I said. "Hopefully we can get her some help. Now, let's get this mess cleaned up. What do you want to do tonight?"

"Petra and Joaquin were having a game night tonight," he said. "I'd like to go for a couple of hours."

I didn't know if Petra and Joaquin were boys or girls, but I also knew that didn't seem to matter to him the way it had to me when I was his age.

"Don't you just do that on the computer?" I asked.

"Board games, Mom," he said. "Real life. In person. Like you always wanted." He grinned. I rolled my eyes.

"Do I know these kids?"

"Sure," he said, and began rattling off things he had done with them and how many times Hayword and I had met their parents.

So we cleaned up the kitchen. Then we hugged—I held him a little too long—and then he left to go play on a school night. I thought that was a good thing: It meant he wasn't worried about school.

As soon as he was gone, I headed out to Fern's apartment. Lance Johnson expected money tomorrow morning or he was publishing all of the photos, including the ones of me and Ryan and me and Hayword. I had to figure what to do about it. Couldn't kill him. I mean, come on, first, it's wrong. Second, I would get caught. Third, it would be messy. Fourth, it was not even an option. I couldn't let those photos get published, but I wasn't going to give him the money. Maybe something in Fern's apartment would explain this entire mess to me.

I still had to write the damn screenplay or lose my company. That seemed the least of it right this moment. But it was my company. Mine and Hayword's. Sally didn't deserve it. Especially with how she was acting now. What did she contribute to the entire enterprise except kissing up to people with money?

Traffic was a bitch from hell.

And not the good kind.

Soon enough I was at Fern's apartment building and then in her apartment. I had only been a couple of times. Fern liked to keep her private life private. I went up three flights of stairs, unlocked her door, and went inside. Her place was about the size of my bungalow, only narrower. She had a view of another apartment building. She said she liked it that way. It reminded her that she was in the movie business—like *Rear Window*—and that Nature didn't really count for anything. I think she said stuff like that just to worry David and piss me off. It didn't piss me off. I thought it was sad.

The place smelled stale. I opened the sliding glass doors to the balcony. Heard the cacophony of traffic. But a breeze wafted in. I sighed and looked around. My stomach felt like it was in a million knots. Fern hardly had any pictures on the walls. It looked more like a hotel room than someone's home. It was so generic.

What had happened to my daughter? When she was younger she had been creative. She was always a pain in the ass. Always argued. Pushed me about everything. But she always made a place her own. We would go to a restaurant, and she would draw pictures and put them up in the booth. "This is my booth," she would say. Or if we went to a park, she would gather sticks and build a little fort, marking out her place in it. Her room in our first house was gorgeous. She picked out the rich maroon paint, made her bed like something out of the *Arabian Nights* and sometimes pretended she was Scheherazade.

Then Alberto died. The house burned down. We moved. I blinked. I couldn't remember much more about her except that she was angry with me. Everything was always my fault. After a while, I just could not stand being in the same room with her.

And vice versa.

But I had thought much of that was healed. Especially after

she started working at Back to Life Studios and helping to run the Foundation. She seemed to have come into her own.

At least, she didn't seem to be blaming me for everything. Maybe that's all I noticed or cared about. Phew: I was out of the line of fire.

Only, apparently I had been mistaken about that.

I began looking through her drawers. I didn't know what I expected to find. I wanted to fix this Lance Johnson problem without her help. Without talking to her. I knew that I would have to talk to her eventually. But right now, I detested her. Right now, I wished she had died instead of Alberto.

I sucked in my breath and slammed shut the drawer I was rummaging through. No, no, no. I didn't wish her dead. That wasn't what I meant. I only meant . . . I don't know what I meant, but I didn't want her dead. Couldn't she just love me and accept me? She loved and accepted her father, and he was a flawed human being too.

I went to her bedroom. Pulled open all her drawers. Found clothes. Looked in her closet. Clothes and shoes. Where was her computer? Didn't she have bills? Paper? Did they do everything online these days?

I left her room and walked down the hallway to the second bedroom. The door was closed and locked. I shook the handle. I was about to try and kick it in—wouldn't that feel great?—when I remembered I had Fern's keys. I fished them out and tried them in the door, one by one. A small one popped open the lock and the door swung open. I had thought it was a guest room, but it looked like her office. Neat and tidy.

I sat at her desk and opened her laptop. Her emails were boring, mostly about work. Nothing to or from Jonathan or Lance Johnson. I looked in her photos. Pictures of her and Jonathan together: eating, laughing, walking on the beach. Maybe she had really liked him.

She had a bunch of folders on her desktop. One was labelled "cat." She didn't have a cat, so I opened it. It was full of about 100 photos of her and Jonathan having sex. I felt sick to my stomach. I closed it. One file was labeled insurance. I clicked on it. 50 photos. I clicked on the first photo. It was Fern naked again. Gawd. Only this time the man under her and later over her was Lance Johnson.

If she had photos of her and Johnson together as insurance why hadn't she shown them to him to get him to not publish the photos?

My head and soul hurt. I sent the file to my email, and then I printed off a few of the photos where Lance's face was very clear. I folded them and put them in my purse.

Then I went to the closet and opened it. I was so surprised that I stepped back.

"What the hell?"

Inside the closet was display shelving, and on those shelves were leather purses. About ten of them. Most of them were pastel-colored or sea colors. A few were round with flat bottoms. The rest were just like regular purses, bags, clutches with handles. I didn't know what to call them. I didn't know anything about such things except that these bags were Persephone bags made by Neptune—I guess that was what the designer called herself now. These purses cost a mint. Some were $20,000 each. Maybe more. I was looking at $200,000 worth of purses that looked like they had never been used. I picked up a light green one—sea foam green? It felt heavy. I took it over to Fern's desk, set it down, and then opened it. Inside this perfect looking bag were tiny bottles of liquor, like the ones Ryan and I had recently drained. Vodka. Brandy. Whiskey. Some wine.

I zipped the purse up again, set it back in its place, and grabbed another purse. This one was magenta-colored and it snapped open. It was stuffed with liquor, too.

It turned out all the purses were filled with small liquor bottles.

I sat in the stuffed chair she had in the room. What could this possibly mean? Had my daughter gone crazy? Why hadn't I wondered that when she secretly gave me liquor and filmed me having sex? And pretended to be dead. I still wasn't sure about that. Had she been dead or not?

I called Hayword.

"Hey," he said. "You OK?"

"No," I said. "You?"

"She's not going into rehab," Hayword said. "She wants to come home and explain it all."

I laughed. "Do you think there's another explanation besides the one where she wants to destroy my life?"

"I would say that not everything is about you," Hayword said, "except that it does appear to be all about you this time."

"I found $20,000 handbags in her closet," I said. "Ten of them. All filled with liquor bottles."

Hayword was silent for a few moments. Then he whispered, "She seems so normal."

"Are you in the room with her?" I asked.

"No," he said, "I got separate rooms."

"Good," I said. "Keep your door locked, and don't give her a key to your room. I don't trust her."

"You think she would try to hurt one of us?" Hayword asked.

"She already has," I said. "I'm just trying to lessen the damage. Talk to you tomorrow."

I rubbed my face. I was still shocked that Fern had spiked my cider. And I was still shocked that I had helped Ryan fall off the wagon. I had pushed him off. My rage at what he had done to me all those years ago—deserting me when I was pregnant with Alberto—didn't give me the right to destroy his life.

I made a noise. I had to make it right. Or something.

I closed Fern's closet. Then I turned off all the lights in her apartment, and I left. I drove to Ryan's house. When he opened the door, he smiled wanly. Then he said, "Hello, you. Devil or demon this time?"

"Come on," I said. "Let's go to a meeting. There's one starting soon."

"Isn't there always?" He came outside and closed the door to his house, locked it. We walked together to my car.

"Maybe after we'll go for coffee," I said, "and I'll show you pictures of Alberto. He kind of looked like you."

"Really?" Ryan said. "How could you tell? He was just a baby."

"Yeah, that's right," I said. "Just like you."

Ryan laughed. And choked a little. And laughed some more. I smiled. God. How we destroy each other little by little and then all at once.

CHAPTER FOURTEEN

Ryan and I walked down the long stairway to the basement of the church that I had not been in since I had seen Ryan there several years earlier. When I had eviscerated him in front of an entire room of recovering alcoholics. That had not been a good night.

Now here we were again after all those years.

When we reached the large meeting room, Ryan took my hand and squeezed it, just for a moment, but long enough for Mark to see it. Yes, my Mark. What was wrong with my brain? This was also where Mark went to AA meetings. It was near his house. He knew Ryan—as Bryan. They used to play in a neighborhood basketball team together.

Ryan went down a row to grab a seat. I smiled at Mark and gave him a hug.

"Are you and Bryan friends now?" Mark asked.

"It's a long story," I said. "He drank again, so I said I'd take him to a meeting."

"I didn't know you were in touch with him," Mark said. "I thought you hated his guts."

I sighed. Fuck. I did not want to explain my life to him or anyone right now.

"Are you all right?" I asked.

He looked good. He was cleaned up. Appeared to be sober.

"I found your key yesterday morning," he said. "Is that your way of saying we're over?"

I glanced at Ryan. He was watching us. He nodded to Mark and started to get up. I waved him away. Then I took Mark's arm. We left the room, walked down the hall, and went into a smaller empty room. I sat on a wooden bench against the wall. He sat next to me but not close.

"I shouldn't have cheated," he said, "but shouldn't we have talked about it before you decided we were finished? You just left me."

"I left you a long time ago. You just didn't notice."

He frowned. "I thought we were just figuring things out. I went back to my job. You went back to the bungalow."

"Didn't that tell you anything?" I asked. "We were moving apart not together."

"You made it seem like it was nothing," he said.

"Because I'm an asshole," I said. "I can't be alone. I don't know how to say goodbye. I don't know how to be close. We were over as soon as we went to live at the beach. It just took a while. We were not living our dreams, neither one of us. You did the restaurant for me, and I thought I wanted to be at the beach. Turns out, I didn't."

"Brooke, I don't care where we are as long as we're together," he said.

I smiled. "You know that's not true. You didn't like it at the beach. You missed your house and your mother and your neighbors. You're more social than I am."

He looked at his hands. I stared at the line of his jaw. It was so beautiful.

"Do you remember the time you pulled Joanie's toe out of the faucet?" I asked.

"I didn't pull it out," he said. "You did."

I laughed. "That's right. She was trying to seduce you. I didn't blame her, of course."

Mark looked at me. "Are you flirting with me?"

"No," I said. "At least, I don't mean to. I was just remembering our beginnings. We had a lot of drunken sex. You were really a good guy."

"You were drunk," he said. "I wasn't. If I were really a good guy, I guess I would have talked you into going to a meeting back then."

"Like anyone could ever talk me into anything," I said. "Well, maybe David. My son does have some sway with me."

"Not Fern?"

I shook my head. "The truth is that I like my life with my kids." OK, with my kid. "And Hayword. I like my job or my work. I think I can do it now and stay sober. I'm not a Hollywood lifer, but I like movies. I like stories. I like being able to create happy endings somewhere, since I can't seem to do it in my own life."

"I'm OK with that," he said.

"You hated all of that," I said. "Really, I think what we liked was fucking one another, especially when I was drunk. That's about all we had in common. Plus, you are such a decent and good man. I liked your company."

"I'm sorry I slept with my ex-wife," he said.

"I'm sorry I didn't know how to say goodbye," I said, "but you do. You did the one thing you knew I couldn't . . . forgive."

"So this is it?" he said, looking around. "After everything we've been through."

I wanted to cry or scream.

"I'm not really in touch with my feelings right now," I said. "Or possibly ever. But I've got so many things going on now with Fern and the business. This feels like the end." I shrugged. "But what do I know?"

Talk about hedging my bets.

"Are you and Ryan a couple now?" he asked.

"No!" I said, a little too forcefully. "No," I said more quietly. "He told me he's had a rough time since that night when I ripped him a new one here. I feel I've got some responsibility for him."

"You don't," Mark said.

He didn't know the whole story, of course. People relapsed when they kept too many secrets, and I had a boatload of them.

"Do you want to fuck one more time?" I asked. "In the bathroom? Or here? Could lock the door. Or keep it unlocked for old time's sake."

Mark laughed. Or chuckled. It wasn't sincere.

"Maybe later," Mark said.

This time, I laughed. "Yikes. A maybe later fuck. That's cold, bro."

We both stood and put our arms around each other.

"If you ever need anything," Mark said.

"You, too," I said.

We let each other go. Mark left the room.

I sat on the bench again. I didn't know if I was relieved or sad. I put my head in my hands.

"Mac?"

I looked up. Ryan was standing next to me.

"On little cat feet?" I asked. "I didn't hear you."

"I followed you down here," he said. "In case there was trouble. Don't worry. Mark didn't see me. You all right?"

He looked so concerned. So gorgeous. He reminded me of

himself all those years ago. Except different. I didn't think the old Ryan was ever concerned about anyone but himself.

He leaned down and kissed me. I wanted to push him away. Instead, I stood up and pressed myself against his body. It was a long slow lovely kiss. I pulled away and went to the door, shut it, and locked it. Ryan was looking around.

"What are you looking for?"

"A bed or a cot?"

"Fucking me up against the wall won't do it?"

"My back has been acting up," he said.

"Oh for fuck's sake," I said. "Don't tell me that."

We found yoga mats and cushions. Soon we were naked—I used my clothes as a mini-sheet so I had something between me and the yoga mats. I didn't know where they'd been.

"Condom," I said, holding out my hand.

"Come on," Ryan said.

"There's the old selfish Ryan," I said. "I don't know where your dick has been. No condom, no sex."

"My dick has been in you," he said. "Remember? I've been impotent for years."

Oh yeah.

I wanted him. He looked delicious in the semi-darkness. I also wanted to stop. Before, I could explain fucking him because I was drunk. I was sober as a mouse now. Or a judge. How would I explain this to anyone?

"I'm not getting pregnant again," I said.

"Aren't you a little old to get pregnant?" Ryan asked.

"Are you trying to get laid or punched?" I asked. "And yes, my eggs probably would be a little old now."

"I don't carry condoms around with me," he said.

I got up, still naked, and grabbed my purse. I dug around in it until I came up with a condom.

Then we got busy.

It was great. He thought I was amazing, beautiful, my cunt perfect. He was so fucking needy, and what he needed was me.

"I can't get sober without you," he said.

"I'm losing my hardon here," I said. "Less talking and more dicking."

I orgasmed. It was nice.

But it had been better when I was drunk.

I wanted to ask Ryan: What do you think? Was it better doing it drunk or sober? But I didn't. I didn't want to do anything to encourage his drinking.

Afterward, we put on our clothes and stayed on the mats. I turned on the lights and then got my phone. I found my photos of Alberto and showed them to Ryan.

"Whenever I get a new phone," I said, "I move the photos. It's not always easy. But I want to have them with me."

We looked through the pictures together. Alberto was young, of course, a baby. So he didn't look that different from one photo to another, at least not to a stranger.

"He's getting his own personality in this photo," Ryan said.

I smiled. "Yep. Seven months old." One month before he died.

"He does have my smile," Ryan said. He looked at me. "He *did* have my smile."

I nodded.

"Do you have photos of your other children?" he asked.

"Sure," I said. "Here's one where Fern is holding Alberto. And here's one of David at school last week. I have lots in-between." I scrolled through the photos. I did have lots of photos of David but very few of Fern.

"My daughter and I don't get along well," I said. "She's causing quite a lot of problems right now."

"I wish I had had a family," he said. "Fifteen years ago it seemed like a horrible idea. Now, I wish I'd done it."

"You had your chance," I said. I put my phone away.

"Really?" he said. "You would have left Hayword and lived with me, with your other two kids? You think we would have made it? Because I don't. I was obviously a selfish bastard. And neither of us had any money."

I nodded. "It would not have been a good thing. In retrospect, I see that. But at the time I was so hurt by it. When Alberto died, I felt like my grief over you leaving me had killed him. I thought I had loved you too much."

"You *thought* you loved me? What does that mean?"

"I'm feeling this concrete floor on my ass," I said. We both stood and began putting the mats and cushions away. "I think what I loved was how free I was with you. By that time, I was stiff with Hayword. I felt like he wanted me to fix everything for him, and I couldn't. So many men seem to want women to be their emotional support animals, and we're not all equipped to do that. I am an emotional kick your ass animal. With you, I could fuck your brains out and then that was it. Getting pregnant just made you another husband. I didn't want that."

I was realizing this all as I said it. The same thing had happened with Mark. Once we were settled down, he was another husband who needed me to be his emotional support person. Fuck that. I had my own problems. I laughed out loud at myself.

"What?" Ryan asked.

"I am such an asshole," I said.

Ryan held out his hand to me. "Welcome to the club," he said.

We skipped the rest of the AA meeting, and I dropped Ryan off at his house.

"You coming in?" Ryan asked as he got out of the car.

"No, David's waiting for me at home," I said, staying in the driver's seat.

"I'd love to meet him," Ryan said. He stood a few feet from the car, looking in at me. "All grown up."

"Maybe," I said, "someday. Right now I have some fires to put out."

"Don't look at me to help you put out fire," he said. "I just inflame; I don't tame." He started laughing as he said it, and I laughed, too.

"Maybe you should take up screenwriting," I said. "What a cornball."

"I actually have started writing," he said. "I'm a lot smarter than I look."

"I doubt that." I grinned. "See you later, gator." Oops. It just slipped out.

"After while, crocodile." He turned and went toward the house.

"Bye, bye, butterfly," I said to myself. As I started to drive away, the phone bleeped or farted or chimed. I put the car in park again and looked at the text. It was from Sally.

"How is that whore of a daughter?" she asked.

"Fucking bitch," I said. "You leave my daughter out of this."

"Has she fucked anyone else's husband today? And speaking of today, how is the script coming? Tick-tock. By the way, Lance Johnson contacted me. Asked if I wanted to buy photos of you fucking some guy in a car. That would be Ryan Nichols, eh? Lance wouldn't email them to me. But he is coming to the office tomorrow afternoon to show me. I bet Hayword would be interested in seeing them. After that, he would want you out of the company, too. Let me know how the script goes."

"Fuck, fuck, fuck," I said as I finished reading the text. I felt like I was going to explode. I imagined my pieces all over the car.

I called our lawyer, Mercy Price. I actually got through to her.

"I need you to go over our contract with Sally St. James," I said. "I want to get rid of her, legally, of course."

"You don't need to qualify that," Mercy said. "Well, unless you do. What's going on?"

"I'll try to make it short," I said. "Fern had sex with Sally's husband, and Sally is enraged. The third script for the *Beauty and the Zombie* film is due in a few days. I haven't started it. If I don't have it finished by Monday, Sally can say I violated the contract, and the punishment for that is I'm no longer a partner, and she and Hayword get the profits for the last two movies, the profits we had."

"I remember," Mercy said. "I advised against that."

"Yes, I know. You were right."

"Are you going to finish the script?" she asked.

"I don't know," I said. "I hope so but lots of things are going on. For one thing, Sally hinted that she is going to show some photos to Hayword, photos of me in flagrante delicto, as it were. Isn't there something in the contract about a morals clause? Isn't blackmail immoral?"

"She's going to do what?" Mercy asked. "Good grief. Are you and Hayword back together?"

"No. We're not back together. She's lashing out. And I want to use that to try and get her out of the company. She wants me out. But it's my fucking company. Mine and Hayword's. We invited her in. I want her out."

"Forward me the text," Mercy said. "I doubt that it's anything actionable. But I'll look over the contract again. Could you buy her out? Remember, any three of you can get dissolve the business as long as nothing is owed. In other words, you can't dissolve it right now because you owe the company a script. But she could say hasta la vista at any time because she isn't obligated to provide the business with anything."

"I don't think we have enough money to buy her out," I said.

"Let me do some discreet nosing around," Mercy said. "Maybe someone needs a studio head, and we could convince them to make Sally an offer. Is there anyone in town who really likes you?"

"Not in particular," I said. "Oh, you're asking me if I've fucked anyone who might do me a favor."

"You got it, sistah," she said. "I call it the Vagina Club. Whoever has been in my veejay is part of the club. I love them all and use them as contacts now and again."

"You mean you fuck people so you can use them as a contact later? That sounds nasty."

"No," Mercy said. "I don't do that. I'm just saying that if he or she has been in the vee, they are still a part of me."

I laughed. "So you're asking me to have a vagina dialogue."

Mercy groaned. "Whatever. Get back with me."

I turned the phone off and threw it in the backseat. Shit. I had forgotten to ask her about Fern embezzling from the Foundation. There was always later.

Man, this felt like one of the longest days of my life in one of the longest weeks of my life.

In reality, the shit storm clusterfuck of a week was only just getting started.

CHAPTER FIFTEEN

David was in bed asleep when I finally got home. I gave him a sloppy kiss on the cheek to wake him up. He laughed and waved me away.

"I love you," I said.

"You, too."

"Hey, David," I said as I sat on the edge of his bed.

"Mom, I've got school in the morning," he mumbled.

"Do you remember me saying goodnight to you when you were a kid?" I asked. "Like something we did every night. See you later, alligator. After while, crocodile. Etc."

He turned toward me but kept his eyes closed.

"No," he said. "That's from your movie *Love and Other Insanities*."

"The other night Fern asked me to say that with her," she said, "like we used to do when she was a kid. Only I never did that with her."

"You did with Alberto," he said. "Not that I remember."

He was a baby himself when Alberto was born.

"But Fern told me," he said. "She said you would do both sides. See you later, alligator and after while, crocodile. To teach it to Alberto. She said you had rituals with him but nothing like that with us. One of her many resentments."

How could I not remember that?

"Don't worry about it, Mom," David mumbled. "She'll get over it." He turned away from me. I patted his hip.

"She hasn't gotten over it yet," I said.

I went to Hayword's office and sat in it for a long time, staring at the computer, looking at websites for movie studios. I did not recognize a lot of the names. Of course, I wasn't on the party circuit.

Who did I know that might offer Sally a job?

I didn't know many suits. I was not very good at small talk, which was ridiculous. Any good socialized adult should be able to talk about nothing. In LA, it was difficult to talk about the weather. "It sure is hot, sunny, and polluted." Or "It sure is hot, sunny, windy, and polluted." Besides, talking about the weather these days just brought up images of the end of the world and how we were all pretty much fucked. Like for instance, the lightning storm which supposedly was on its way here. Just another one of those maybe things.

No. I wasn't going to go down that rabbit hole. I needed to think about who could help me get rid of Sally.

I should have been a better person over the years. Or I should have had sex with more powerful people. The only stud head I had ever fucked was Sally.

Maybe if I was nice to her now.

I pulled out my phone and texted, "Should have the script to you soon. I am so sorry about all of this with Fern. Please let me know if I can do anything to make it right."

I got an immediate reply. That was hopeful. I looked down at the text. "You can drop dead."

I set the phone down. "Well, I don't see how me dropping dead could help but thanks for the sentiment. Jesus," I said aloud to no one.

I did know two studio heads: Katherine and Oscar Bernstein of OK Studios. Maybe this was why I had dreamed about them. The Universe was giving me a heads-up. Sally had said she wished she had their catalog. They always loved Hayword and me. Maybe they could hire Sally away from Back to Life Studios as a favor to us.

I remembered Oscar had a cornball sense of humor, which was strange given he was from New York originally. When I first met him, I asked him about the name of their studio. He shrugged and said, "You know, we're not great and we're not terrible. We're OK."

Hayword had loved that. In truth, O and K were the initials of their first names.

Just then Phil phoned. When I answered it, he said, "I figured out who put the list up. It was easy as pie. Although I don't know how to make pie."

"Old joke, old man," I said.

He laughed. "Gee, thanks. It was Fern. I bet that's no surprise to you. She did not cover her tracks. I don't know why she did it."

I sighed. "I think she wants to destroy me. I don't understand. I wasn't that bad of a mother."

"Have you talked to her yet?" Phil asked.

"No, they're coming home tomorrow," I said. "That is when the shit will hit the fan. Hey, you asked me to tell you, so I'm telling you. I'm going to Lance Johnson's office tomorrow."

"To do what?"

"To talk," I said. "To talk him out of blackmail. To keep those photos out of the press."

"I asked a friend to run a background check on him," Phil said. "He's a bad dude. When he was younger, he was jailed for auto theft, check fraud, and assault."

"Anything lately?" I asked.

"No. He married, got holy. His wife has a little money that keeps them all going."

"I can handle him," I said.

"Let me come with you," Phil said.

"That sounds like a good idea," I said. "I pretended I was Fern—cuz I have her phone—and said I'd meet him at his office at 10:00. He thinks he's meeting Fern. I'll be there a few minutes early and I'll look for you."

"Sounds like a plan."

We said our good nights.

I was exhausted. I felt weird sleeping in Hayword's bed, especially right after having sex with his nemesis. Not that he would call Ryan that. What would he call him? Alberto's father. He didn't have anything against Ryan. Still he would be hurt that I had had sex with him again. Especially given . . . I had just been with him.

What was it with people and sex? I didn't really understand it. I could not remember or count how many people I had fucked. While I was married. Yet Hayword cheated on me once, and I never trusted him again.

Lately, it hadn't seemed so important.

I put my head in my hands. Too much was going on. I had fucked it all up. I couldn't fix it. Ryan and I were both drinking. Mark was drinking. Fern was whatever Fern was. My friendships with Sally and Joanie were over. Oh, fuck, I had forgotten about Joanie and her dead husband. I hoped she had called the police. If it wasn't for David being here, I would go to Ryan's house now. Why? Why? Why?

It was all Fern's fault.

I went downstairs to the kitchen. I opened the cupboard where I knew Hayword kept the wine. I pulled down a bottle of red wine. From Chateaux Who Gives a Fuck as long as there is alcohol in it. Then I looked around for the corkscrew. Couldn't find it.

"Fuck, fuck, fuck."

I breathed deeply. Breathed again. David was upstairs. My son was upstairs. I couldn't do this. Could not do this again.

I opened another cupboard. Where the chocolate was. I got a bar of 97% dark cacao. I unwrapped the bar and shoved half of it in my mouth and began to chew. I leaned against the counter and closed my eyes.

"You left a little chocolate out of your mouth."

I opened my eyes. My sleepy-looking son stood in the kitchen.

I took the chocolate bar out of my mouth and held it out to him. "You want some?"

David waved me away. "Gross! And it's all over your mouth."

I laughed, turned around, and washed my mouth in the sink. When I turned around again, David was looking at the wine bottle.

"Don't worry," I said. "I didn't drink any."

I picked it up and put it in the cupboard.

"I couldn't find the damn corkscrew," I said. "Man, sometimes I just wish I was like everyone else." I let out a little scream.

"Me, too," he said. "I mean I wish I was like everyone else. But everyone is fucked up, Mom. They just pretend better than we do."

I went over to him and put my arms around him. He returned the embrace. "I hope you're not fucked up," I said. "And quit swearing."

"I'm not as fucked up as Fern at least," he said.

"You are not."

"Do you ever wonder what Alberto would be like now?" he asked.

"All the time," I said. "I bet he'd be a lot like you, and you'd be great pals to each other."

"Or maybe he would have been pals with Fern," David said. "I think she really needs one."

"You're a good kid," I said. "Now that I have all of this chocolate revving me up, let's go to sleep."

I fell asleep on Hayword's bed. On top of the covers. I slept right through David leaving for school. He texted me his love. I went to the bungalow, took a shower, changed my clothes. Then I drove to Lance Johnson's office which was way on the other side of town, in a place I had never been before. Fern sure knew how to pick them.

I parked. Everything depended upon these next moments. And then the moments after that.

"Let's do this thing," I said to no one.

I saw Phil as I got out of the car, walking toward me.

"What are you going to do?" Phil asked when he was next to me.

"You'll see," I said. "Don't worry. I didn't bring a gun."

"I did," Phil said.

"I wish you hadn't told me that."

"I'm trained," he said. "No one is gonna get hurt."

"Said almost everyone who hurt someone with a gun."

We went inside the square brick office building. Johnson's office was on the first floor. We went to his huge steel door. I didn't know if I should knock or just go in. I opened the door.

Inside was a tiny office with just a few chairs and another closed door. I didn't have time to think about it because Lance Johnson came walking through the back door.

"Oh, fuck," he said when he saw us. "Not you again. And the mother. I've seen your ass all over the little screen." He grinned like he wasn't afraid of anything. I wanted to punch him.

"I know about your little scheme with my daughter," I said. "I know that Sally St. James isn't going to pay you anything. I know that you have photos of me having sex. Illegally obtained, by the way. I didn't give you permission to come into my house or my car. I could have you charged with breaking and entering."

"Your daughter had a key," he said. "Besides, I can give you those photos back. Along with the memory card. Just give me the money."

"Let's see them," I said. "I want to see the photos and the memory cards for my car and house and for Fern with Jonathan."

Johnson shrugged. "As long as you have your checkbook." He turned around and headed for the back. I looked at Phil.

"I'll be coming with you," Phil said.

"No one goes back here," Johnson said.

"Mr. Case is a retired police officer," I said. "Did you know that? He is obligated to report any unlawful activities. And I would say that all of your activities regarding me and my daughter are unlawful. He's going back with you."

Johnson fussed for a bit, but Phil followed. They left the door open. I heard very little chatter. After what seemed like forever, they came back. Johnson looked pissed. Phil showed me the memory cards.

"We took the photos off his computer, too," Phil said. "And the cloud. I looked through his mail and his phone. I didn't see any more, but he probably has a stash somewhere. I've got the memory cards."

"You owe me for those," Johnson said.

"I don't owe you a thing," I said. "Well, except for these." I pulled the photos out of my bag, unfolded them, and handed them to Johnson. "I know that you're a Christian man now with a wife who is dedicated to her church, a wife who brings in most of the money. If she saw these, my guess is that your marriage would be in trouble. I wouldn't want that to happen. So I will keep copies of these, and no one else will ever know about them unless any of the photos you took of me or of Fern see the light of day. If that happens, I will personally hand these photos of you fucking my daughter over to your wife."

Johnson looked away from the photos. "I'll just tell her they're fakes. She believes any bullshit I tell her."

I nodded. "I bet she does. I can always bring Fern with me, to verify that you were fucking her."

"You would do that to your daughter?" Johnson asked.

"Given what you two were trying to do to me, I think you know the answer to that. Do we have a deal, Mr. Johnson?"

He grumbled and shifted. "I'm not getting anything out of this."

"You're not getting your life destroyed," I said. "I can't say the same thing."

"All right," Johnson said. "All right."

I snatched the photos from him. "I hope I never see you again."

I left the office. I could hear Phil behind me. We went outside into the sunshine, and I turned to Phil. He held out his hand to me, and I shook it.

"Man, I don't want to get on your bad side."

"You do not," I said. "This *was* easy as pie, my friend. I have dealt with assholes like him before. Now I need to go and deal with the asshole I gave birth to."

CHAPTER SIXTEEN

I did not want to say goodbye to Phil or drive back to the house where Hayword and Fern would be fairly soon. Maybe I should make them come to the bungalow, and we could have it out there. No, Fern and I had had it out at the bungalow a couple of times. No need for another round there.

I pulled off to the side of the road and looked on the contacts on my phone for Katherine and Oscar or OK Studios. Nothing. I phoned our studio. Caryn answered the phone.

"Hi, Caryn," I said. "Thanks for figuring out what was going on with that list with Phil."

"It was shocking," Caryn said. "Your own daughter. Jesus."

"Yeah, I doubt Jesus had anything to do with it."

"I heard she's fired."

"Did you hear why?" I asked.

"I know why," Caryn said. "You really should not have sex with the boss's husband."

"No, shit," I said.

"Have you finished the script?" Caryn asked, whispering.

"Not yet," I said, "but don't tell anyone."

"I'm rooting for you," she said.

"I need to ask you for a name and phone number, but please don't tell anyone I asked."

"Of course," she said. "I would do anything for you. Well, not anything. But you know what I mean."

I laughed. "This *is* Hollywood, but I think I know what you mean. Do you have the phone number for OK Studios and/or Katherine and Oscar Bernstein? Their unlisted private number."

"Hang on," she said. "Got it. I'll text it to you."

"Thanks," I said. "I'll be in touch."

As soon as I got the text, I called Katherine and Oscar. I heard Katherine's bright friendly voice say, "Hello, darlin'! I haven't heard from you in ages. How's it going?"

"Hi, Katherine," I said. "Sorry to be so long gone. Can I come see you two? I want to talk about something."

"Sure," Katherine said. "We live out a bit on a few acres. You up for that?"

"Of course," I said.

"I'll text you the address," she said. "Come to the house, not the Hex Barn. See you soon, darlin'."

The Hex Barn?

I clapped my hands together. Yes. I adored these people. Why had I cut them out of my life? To be fair, I had pretty much cut everyone out of my life from the before-Alberto-died time. But that was all in the past. Maybe now they could provide a solution to my Sally problem. Plus I could delay dealing with Fern.

I texted Hayword and asked when they would be home. He answered, "One to three hours, depending upon the traffic."

That gave me time.

I checked my other texts. David wrote, "Storm will hit this

afternoon. I'm coming home early from school." I looked up. Sky was still blue.

I drove away from our village and up into the hills and beyond. I didn't think I had been out this way before. I felt myself relaxing as I drove through the green rolling hills. Maybe it would be OK, OK, OK. What would it have been like if the kids had been raised out here? Would they have been happier, healthier? Would Hayword and I have been happier, healthier? Would we still be together?

No. I was not going to do that. Too many questions with too few answers. That way led to me taking another drink.

Soon enough, I turned down a dirt road and then down a dirt driveway. Tall sycamores sheltered the road for most of the way. Just before I got to the house, the trees made way for huge rhododendron bushes and then butterfly bushes and thousands of California poppies that led me to the house. I parked alongside two other cars. To my left was a big red barn with a huge Pennsylvania Dutch hex sign of a rooster on it.

"Ah, the Hex Barn."

To my right was a path that led to what looked like a true California Ranch house, golden, one story, hugging the ground. Big old white oak trees towered over one end of the house. All kinds of flowering bushes leaned forward along the front, not blocking the many large windows. Out front on the porch under the overhanging roof and several sycamores, Katherine and Oscar sat at a wooden table and chairs. They both stood and waved when they saw me.

I hurried toward them. Katherine's hair was now long and white. She was so beautiful. Oscar was still short and stout with salt and pepper hair. They both embraced me.

"You haven't aged a bit," Katherine said. "You were always so darling."

I laughed. "And you two were and are always beautiful."

"Sit with us in the shade," Oscar said. "Have some tea." He poured iced tea into an empty glass for me.

"This place is absolutely gorgeous," I said. I breathed deeply. It was the first deep breath I had had in a long while. "Is your studio here or do you just live here?"

"We've lived here for nearly twenty years now," Katherine said. "The studio has been here about ten years in the Hex Barn. We have a couple other houses on the property that we use in our films. We live by the threes."

"The threes?" I asked.

"We told you about it," Oscar said, "when we produced *Love and Other Insanities*. We had just started it then."

I shrugged. "I've forgotten. Sorry."

Katherine said, "We give three hours a day to the land, three hours to our work, and three hours to our community. We've had a lot of privilege in our lives, we know. So we try to give back."

"We have 500 hundred acres now," Oscar said.

"Wow," I said. "The trees, the house, all the birds I hear. It's paradise." Of course, I used to think the same about the beach. I would probably be bored here, too, even though right this second, it felt like . . . home.

"We owe it all to you," Katherine said. "Without *Love and Other Insanities* we probably would have never bought this place."

"Because of the money?" I asked.

Katherine shrugged. "That and because it was such a beautiful tender movie about the value of family over work. We were looking for a house closer in for the kids, but we came here, and we fell in love. The kids loved it, too. They're all grown up now, have their own kids. How are Fern and David?"

"David is fine," I said, "but Fern has been trouble. That's why I'm here."

"First, drink your tea," Katherine said. "And then we will

show you the house. Did you hear about this lightning storm coming today?"

"I have indeed," I said.

I drank the tea. They talked about their grandchildren while I listened and looked around. I felt that familiar flutter I got when I was around other people, but it began to dissipate as I sat there under the big trees.

"This place was built by a Spanish rancher," Oscar said. "I forget what year. But she was a woman. Francesca Morales."

"She had more names than that," Katherine said.

"I know, but I can never remember them," Oscar said.

Katherine said, "Me, neither. Sorry Francesca. It's cultural."

"Anyway. She raised horses. People came from all around the world to buy her horses. Her husband was a painter. They had five children. She oversaw every part of the building of this house. She wanted it always filled with family and friends."

"It has so much natural light," Katherine said. "And the courtyard is right out of a story."

"It burned to the ground in the eighties," Oscar said, "but the owners—who were her descendants—rebuilt it from the original specs. We still don't know how they did that. They used local materials just as she had. But they modernized it, thank goodness. Come. We'll show you."

They took me inside. The Great Room had a vaulted ceiling with a chandelier hanging from it. The library on one side of the Great Room had shelves up to the ceiling. The kitchen was huge, with tall cream-colored cabinets. The décor was a mixture of Mexican, Spanish, and Californian: colorful and sedate and neutral all at the same time. We walked down wide hallways and out into a courtyard that was filled with flowers, as though the courtyard was a vase and every flower in the world had been stuffed into it. It smelled like lavender mixed with roses mixed with lilacs, only not overwhelming. Above was open to the California sun.

"Oh my word!" I said. "This is amazing."

"Katherine has the greenest thumb in the world," Oscar said.

"Not a single artificial chemical used here," Katherine said. "Come, sit here." She pointed to a long wooden table in the middle of the courtyard: the only place without flowers. Carved in the center of the table were the words: *There's no place like home.* Katherine and I sat on opposite benches. Oscar disappeared for a minute and then reappeared with a plate full of sandwiches.

"Tell us everything," Oscar said as he sat down.

So I did. Surrounded by the most beautiful fragrant flower garden I had ever experienced, I told them about my drinking.

"We had heard something," Katherine said.

Then me stopping drinking. Fern and the fake robbers. Fern with a job at Back to Life Studios. And then the photos of her sleeping with Sally's husband. Fern stealing from the Foundation. Sally so angry that she was trying to get me out of Back to Life Studios.

Katherine shook her head. "You've had the troubles."

"That girl needs some help," Oscar said.

"Hayword is bringing her home," I said, "right now. We'll have it out with her tonight."

"During the lightning storm?" Katherine asked.

"I don't know," I said. "I hadn't thought about it."

"That could be bad luck," she said. "Try to do it before."

"Or after," Oscar said.

I smiled. "I heard a rumor that you might be looking for a new studio head. Would you consider Sally?"

Katherine and Oscar looked at each other.

"We are looking to retire," Katherine said. "We want to

move closer to our grandchildren. They live in your village, actually."

"You would leave this place?" I asked.

"500 acres is a lot to manage," Oscar said. "It's time. We're thinking of selling the studio, our catalog, and this place to someone who would really appreciate it."

"Would you consider selling it all to Sally St. James?"

"I don't know," Katherine said. "We didn't really click when we met. But Oscar and I will talk about it. We're not in a rush. We haven't even put out the word yet."

"Oh, thank you," I said. "That is such a relief."

"We said we'd think about it, Brooke," Katherine said, smiling.

"I know," I said, "but these last few days have been so awful that I will grasp at any straw."

"If she bought it," Oscar said, "she would have control over *Love and Other Insanities*."

I groaned. "Way to kill the mood, Oscar," I said. They laughed.

"You'd still have your stake in it," Katherine said. "That is not ours to sell."

"I've got to go," I said. "Fern and Hayword will be back soon."

"Please come back and we'll show you around the entire place," Katherine said.

"I will," I said. "Thank you."

"By the way, we've had a woman living in one of our guest cottages for the last few years," Katherine said. "Terra Lee. She got her psychology degree a couple of years ago, and she's been working as an addiction counselor and a sober companion. She does interventions. She is apparently quite good and very skilled. Unconventional. We adore her. Maybe she can help you with Fern?"

"Oh my word!" I said. "If I believed in angels, I'd say you two are my angels. I haven't seen you in so long and then this week I dreamed about you and someone else mentioned you and now I'm here and you're saving my life. OK, not literally saving my life. But I'm so excited! Yes, please give Terra Lee my contact number. We could use her help. Tell her everything. Tell her anything."

I felt giddy. Like a school girl.

We all stood. I hugged them again. Katherine looked at me. "It's going to be OK," she said.

"Or not," I said. "Alberto was supposed to be OK, but he wasn't. Now Fern. She was dead just a few days ago. I'm so angry with her. And I am absolutely terrified for her. I can't lose two children."

Katherine embraced me again. "You won't, darlin'. You won't."

They walked me out to the car. I got in and drove away, and then I burst into tears. I cried all the way down the driveway and the dirt road. By the time I was out on the main road, I was myself again: my emotions all wrapped up in a ball in my stomach.

CHAPTER SEVENTEEN

I turned on the radio as I headed home. Everywhere, they were talking all about the predicted electric storm.

"Climate change is about to deal us another blow," the radio announcer said. "This storm could rain down thousands of bolts of lightning every second. That's right. Every second. This storm could destroy the city, your home, your car, your future. And it's all your fault. You're listening to this as you're driving your gas-guzzling car, aren't you? Well there you go, asshole."

"What?" I started laughing. "Did he really just say that?"

Blue-black clouds were riding the southwest horizon now. Maybe this storm was going to show up after all.

Then I was back at the house. Hayword's car was in the driveway. I took a deep breath. I was about to get out of the car when my phone beeped. I picked it up and looked at it.

From Ryan. "Stay safe from the storm."

I started to text back, "I am the storm, baby." I laughed out loud. No, I wasn't going to say that. Even if it was true. Instead, I wrote, "You, too."

Then I got out of the car and went into the house.

"We're in here." Hayword's voice. In the living room. I kept walking. David was there.

Fern was sitting next to her father. She looked scared shitless.

Good.

"David, are you sure you want to be here for all of this?" I asked.

He nodded.

"So what the fuck, Fern?" I was so angry I was trembling. Fern looked at her father.

"Don't look to him," I said. "You were trying to ruin my life. You have to answer to me. You spiked my drink. You put cameras in my car and bedroom. You put a list online telling everyone this was a list of men I had slept with. You embezzled money from the Foundation and forged your brother's signature. You could both go to jail!"

I glanced over at David and shook my head almost imperceptibly.

"He won't go to jail," Fern said. "I'll tell them I did it."

"And the worst thing you did, the thing that tells me how much you hate me, is you overdosed so that I would see it. You planned it with Joanie as some kind of sick joke. Do you understand how fucking evil that is?"

Tears flowed down Fern's cheeks.

I didn't believe a single one.

"What do you have to say for yourself?" I asked.

Suddenly the room got darker. David glanced outside.

"It's here," he said.

"We better get the cars in the garages," Hayword said.

"I don't have my keys," Fern said.

I didn't tell her I had them.

"There are only three spots in the garage anyway," Hayword said.

"We'll be right back," I said.

Hayword and I went out into a day that was almost night with black clouds overhead. He got into his car and opened the garage doors. I got into my car, and then we both drove into the garage and parked next to David's car.

"What about Fern's car?" Hayword asked as the garage doors closed on the coming storm.

"Maybe she'll get lucky," I said.

"Don't you think you're being a little rough on her?"

I stared at him.

"OK," he said, putting up his hands.

"I talked to Mercy Price," I said. "She suggested that we find Sally a job too good to refuse and then maybe she'll leave Back to Life Studios on her own accord. Remember any of us can dissolve the partnership at any time for no reason at all, as long as there's nothing else in the pipe—like my script."

"We've got a whole movie about to be made," Hayword said.

I shrugged. "We'd figure something else. I talked to Katherine and Oscar Bernstein today. You were right about their place. It is amazing. They're thinking of selling it and OK Studios with the whole catalog. I bet if they offered it to Sally, she would take it. Then we would be home free. You wouldn't believe how nasty Sally is being. She's threatening all kinds of things."

"Like what?"

The lights went off in the garage. Not a blackout, I didn't think. They stayed on for a bit after the doors closed. Hayword waved his arms around, and they came back on.

"I want to talk to you later about it," I said. "Privately."

"We're pretty private right now," he said.

"Not in the middle of me chewing out Fern."

"What is it? What does Sally have on you."

I leaned against my car, and I looked into Hayword's eyes. His beautiful eyes. It was never my intention to hurt or humiliate him, yet I kept on doing it. Fuck my intentions.

"I saw Ryan Nichols," I said. "I had sex with him. In my car where there was a camera. The blackmailer has photos of that. Sally knows about it, and she threatened to tell you."

"Who you have sex with is your business," Hayword said. "It's nothing to do with me."

I nodded. "It was right after we had had sex. You and me."

"You mean this happened recently?"

"Yes, it happened this week. Monday. I was drinking. I saw him on the way to a meeting and something snapped or clicked, and I wanted to punish him."

"Is that what you were doing with me on Sunday?" he asked. "Were you punishing me by having sex with me?"

"Maybe," I said. "I don't know. It was all crazy. When I drank on Saturday and didn't know it, I think it broke me."

"Isn't that a fine excuse." He shook his head. "I don't know why I'm mad or why it hurts. You didn't promise me anything. You never have. Even when we got married you told me it wasn't what you wanted. You didn't want to be a wife or a mother. You liked the idea of us writing stories together. But Ryan Nichols. Did you really have to fuck him right after you fucked me?"

"I lost my mind. I'm sorry. I don't love him. I don't want to be with him."

"Do you want to be with me?"

"I don't know," I said.

"I didn't even know you and Mark had broken up," Hayword said.

I sighed. "Neither did he."

"I want a divorce," Hayword said.

"What? I thought there wasn't anything I could do that you wouldn't forgive? I thought you would always love me."

"I will," Hayword said. "But this isn't healthy. It's time to make a clean break of it. Same with the studio. As soon as you deliver the manuscript and fulfill your contract, I'm going ask to dissolve the partnership."

"But I love working with you," I said.

Hayword laughed. "Too little, too late, girlie. Let's go fix our daughter before this storm hits."

This was not what I expected. I thought he would be angry and hurt. I didn't think he would be matter of fact. This was the straw that broke the camel's back?

The garage turned dark again. I followed Hayword through the door and into the kitchen and then into the living room.

"Where were we?" Hayword asked.

David was staring outside. It was pitch dark, except when a lightning strike lit up the area. There was one. And then another. And another.

"I unplugged our computers," David said.

"Fern," Hayword said. "Explain yourself. We need to know what your motive was before we turn you over to the police."

I almost laughed out loud. Like Hayword would ever do that.

"Daddy," Fern said. "You can't."

"Don't call me daddy," Hayword said. "You're a grown woman. Act like it."

"I am so sorry for everything I've done," Fern said. "It's the alcohol and the drugs."

"Bullshit," I said. "You have these come to Jesus moments every few years and say you're sorry, and then you get mean and nasty all over again. What the fuck is wrong with you?"

"I don't know!" she said. "You all seem happy and content, and I am not. Mom loved Alberto so much that she left us after he died. He was that special. But we weren't special enough for her to stay with us. Emotionally."

"Give me a break," I said. "You are almost thirty years old. You should be long past your mommy issues. I made sure you had a roof over your head and clothes on your back."

"Those are things!" Fern said. "Where were you? You were drunk or fucking someone!"

"I am so sick of this fucking story," I said. "You had a great childhood. I'm sorry if you don't remember it. Then Alberto died. I drank. Our marriage fell apart. But everything else was good. Why do you focus on the few awful years?"

"I don't know!" she said. "And you've left us this fucked up world."

"Jesus," I said. "And our parents left us a fucked up world, and their parents left them a fucked up world. We've all got shit to overcome. My parents weren't perfect, but I never tried to destroy them!"

"I didn't try to destroy you," Fern said. "I thought you'd get a little drunk, do stupid things, and then you'd get sober again. Easy peasy."

I roared. "First, it isn't up to you to decide that. I did do stupid things. I slept with your father. Then I slept with Ryan Nichols who is trying to stay sober. Lance Johnson wanted to sell those photos to the tabloids. That would have ruined Ryan's life and embarrassed the hell out of us. And Sally is so angry that she wants me out of the company if I can't get the script to her. And I want a drink again more than anything in the world. You destroyed years of hard work."

"I just needed a quick way to make money," Fern said, "and no one would give me any. Sally is such a bitch."

"Do you hear yourself?" I asked. "You sound like a sociopath. You don't give a shit about any of it."

"Because you don't like me!" she shouted. "You have never

fucking liked me. That hurts. If your own mother doesn't like you, it's difficult to stay in the world."

"I have always loved you," I said. "And when you were younger, I liked you. But for the last 15 years, you've treated me like dog shit. Why would I like anyone who treated me that way?"

"Because you're my mother," she said. "You should still like me."

"I don't know who fed you that bullshit," I said. "But parents like or dislike their children just like they like and dislike people who aren't their children. Right now, I like you less than practically anyone. Anyone but Lance Johnson. Oh, by the way, I showed him the photos of the two of you together. He won't be publishing those photos of you and Sally's husband any time soon."

The room was silent. The lights flickered. But they stayed on. Thunder rolled over us and around us, again and again.

"Fern, you have a good job," Hayword said. "Why do you need so much money?"

"I don't know," she said. "Part of it is for drugs. But I've also started this business called More for More. I buy very expensive items and then I sell them for more. I take them to a party or a business meeting where there are famous people, so that I can tell people later where the items have been, and then I jack up the price because of that. People love everything that a celebrity has touched. Or looked at. Breathed on."

"Is that what those handbags are in your closet?" I asked.

"Yes, and they're all spoken for," she said. "All 20% up from retail."

"That's such bullshit," David said. "What is a celebrity? They haven't done anything. They're not better than anyone else. Why would someone pay more for something just because a so-called celebrity has been around it. It's ridiculous. That market is gonna die."

"I hope not," Fern said. "Wait. What were you doing in my closet?"

"Trying to find out why you'd died," I said, "and how I could help you."

I sat in one of the chairs. I was exhausted. I couldn't even remember everything Fern had done wrong to throw in her face.

"And of course, you are fired," I said.

"She can't fire me just because I slept with her husband," Fern said.

I looked at Hayword.

"You can be fired without cause," Hayword said, "but we had plenty of cause to fire you. You have done so many terrible things, Fern. What if your mother had driven after she'd drank your Martinelli's and gotten into an accident and killed someone?"

Fern just sighed.

The house shook with thunder. The outside was lit up from lightning.

"Don't touch any metal," Hayword said, "and don't use the faucets."

"It's pouring down rain," David said as he closed the curtains.

"I am sorry for everything that's happened," Fern said. "I won't do any of it again. I will go to rehab."

"You need to pay back the money you stole from the Foundation," David said. "That's the first thing."

"I don't have any money," Fern said, "particularly now that I'm fired."

"You have those fucking handbags," I said.

"I guess."

Grrr.

"You are a privileged entitled fucking little brat," I said. "If you don't pay back that money, we are going to have you prosecuted and put you in jail."

"OK! I will pay it back."

"By next week," I said. "You'll have to figure out your own rehab. We are not paying for it."

"But I won't have any insurance now that you've fired me," she said.

"Well, now you'll see how the rest of the world lives," I said. "Welcome to real life."

The house shook again. David was looking at his phone. "Downtown LA is on fire. And they're in blackout."

"We've got a generator," Hayword said. "If the power goes out, we'll be OK."

"Isn't that generator full of fuel?" David asked. "It it gets struck by lightning, it'll be like a bomb."

Hayword looked at me and grimaced. He hadn't thought of that—didn't know if it was true.

Just then the doorbell rang. We all looked at one another. In the middle of a once in a lifetime storm?

Hayword and I went to the door. I flung it open.

Eartha Kitten was standing on our doorstep, soaked to the bone. She smiled and held out her hand, "Terra Lee, at your service. I'm here to do one amazing thing a day for you."

CHAPTER EIGHTEEN

I grinned, took Eartha's hand, and pulled her out of the
rain. Laughing, I hugged her.

"You're Terra Lee? Is that your real name?"

"I'll never tell," she said, "but I really did go to school and I
really am an addict specialist. I was in the village when Katherine texted me about your visit. She had no idea we knew each
other. So I came right up."

Hayword was watching and listening and was completely
baffled.

"Eartha lives with Katherine and Oscar, on their property.
She is now a trained addiction specialist, a sober companion.
She's come to talk with Fern."

Eartha and Hayword hugged. Then the kids came in. It took
a second, but then they ran to her and hugged her.

"Oh, David," Eartha said. "You are a young man now.
Amazing. And Fern, so nice to see you. I've heard that you've
tried to ruin your mother's life and you've almost succeeded. Do

you want to talk about how drugs and alcohol are a good choice in your life?"

Fern's mouth fell upon. "This isn't religion, is it?" she asked.

"The religion of healthy sobriety," Eartha said, "if that's what you want. Let's go talk up in your old room. We'll be down in a while."

The three of us were left alone.

"That was a nice bit of synchronicity," Hayword said. "By the way, have you finished the script."

"I haven't even started," I said.

We went back to the living room. I sat on the couch. David picked up his laptop from the table and handed it to me.

"It's fully powered," he said.

"I need some peace and quiet," I said. "I can't do it in the middle of a lightning storm." Just then lightning flashed—could see it through the curtains—and then the electricity went out. After a little bit of time, a few lights came on in the house. The generator was working.

"I can't do it while we're figuring out whether Fern is going to jail or not."

"You've got a lot of excuses," Hayword said. "Like daughter, like mother."

"You can do it, Mom," David said. "We'll help. So the last movie ended with Aiden dead and buried. His mom Colleen visited his grave along with his girlfriend Molly. When they left, his arm came up through the grave. What's next?"

I put my fingers on the keyboard and opened an empty document. Then I typed in *Beauty and the Zombie, Part Three: Whackadoodle Times* by Brooke McMurphy.

As I continued typing, I read it out loud, "The earth breaks open and Aiden pulls himself up out of the grave. The music tells us this is a happy moment, something we have all waited for. But then the camera pans around him, and we see his face, his expression, and we know that this is a different Aiden: this is evil Aiden."

"Good!" David said. "He's alive, but he's a shit."

I looked at Hayword. He nodded. "Keep going."

"What do you think happens next?" I asked, staring at the computer.

"All the dead zombies claw their way out of the graves," David said.

I typed and read, "Aiden pulls off the swan ring his father had given him, the swan ring his mother had given his father, and throws it in the dirt. He stands on his grave looking around, and one arm after another breaks through the earth. Then one by one, the dead alien zombies pull themselves out of the ground. Their graves are all slightly downhill from Aiden. So they look up at him and put their fists in the air in solidarity.

"'The human world has ostracized us!' Aiden shouts. 'They have killed us. This is our planet now! We will show them who is in charge as we drink their blood!'

"We see a human grave-digger begin running away. Aiden shouts, 'Get him,' and the zombies run after him. We hear his screams as they descend on him. Roll credits."

I looked up. David laughed. "All right, Mom!"

"Dead alien zombies begin bursting from their graves all over the world. They are able to telepathically communicate with each other. They go on killing sprees wherever they are. Colleen goes to Aiden's grave and finds it empty and discovers the swan ring. She picks it up and puts it on her finger. She suspects Aiden is part of the murder sprees, but she doesn't know he is the leader. Molly, who is an alien-human mix, finally admits that she has been getting telepathic messages from Aiden. The newly alive dead aliens are particularly interested in getting the mixed children to be a part of their movement. Molly says she hasn't answered Aiden.

"Aiden comes on television and says that the killing will stop if the humans turn over all controls of the government to them. 'You can continue your wasteful consumption,' he says, 'and ruining your environment with fossil fuels. You can do what you want, but we will have the power, and you will do whatever we want.' Most of the people in most of the countries go along with it. They are tired of the killing. The zombie aliens use a portion of the population as their slaves, to serve them and build homes that comfort them."

The house shook again from thunder. Lightning lit up everything. David looked momentarily worried and then he said, "Shouldn't Aiden and Colleen meet?"

I nodded. I kept typing and reading aloud, "Not every reanimated alien zombie is a murderer—although most are—but several of those who aren't come to Colleen and Molly. (Remember they are both scientists.) These alien zombies allow the scientists to examine them. They learn that the reanimated alien zombies are no longer cured of the original zombie illness that brought them to Earth. In fact, the reanimation put the illness into high gear, and it is now deadly. The zombie aliens will die soon if they don't have a cure. Colleen and Molly try the cure from the last movie, but it doesn't work.

"They work night and day trying to find a cure, although they question each other. If the zombie aliens have a deadly disease, why don't they just let them die? Colleen says she can't let Aiden die, no matter how evil he is."

"Aiden could never be evil," Fern said as she walked into the room with Eartha. "He's Alberto, after all."

"He's not Alberto," I said. "We're trying to finish this treatment so I can write the script and save the business. If that happens, then you didn't ruin my life."

"We do need to talk," Eartha said.

"Not yet," Fern said. "Let her finish. So do I gather the zombie aliens are back and they're sick again and Colleen is looking for a cure?"

"Yep," David said.

Thunder shook the house and lightning flashed again.

"Maybe a little lightning à la Frankenstein's monster would do the trick," Fern said.

"Yes!" I said. I continued typing and reading out loud. "One night Molly and Colleen are talking about Frankenstein, and they both have the idea to use electricity on the zombie aliens. They try it on the volunteers, and the disease is arrested. The aliens are disease-free. Yay! Colleen asks Molly to use her ability to communicate with Aiden to let him know they have a cure for the new zombie disease.

"She does and Aiden turns up at the lab. Colleen is choked up and thrilled to see her son. Her boy is alive! What could be more wonderful?"

I stopped typing. The room was quiet again. What an amazing thing that would be, to see her son alive again. I looked up at Hayword. I could see all the pain and grief etched on his face.

I looked down at the computer again. "Colleen embraces Aiden. He lets her, but then she steps back. She explains that they've figured out a cure for the zombie disease that makes them so murderous. She's willing to use the cure on him right then and there. He would go back to being his old compassionate loving self.

"'Why would I want that?' he asks. He refuses treatment. She tells him he will die. 'We all die.' Some of the zombies do come for treatment, and they are cured. However, even after treatment, the zombie aliens begin to die again because, you know, you can't really come back to life.

"Aiden returns to Colleen and begs her to cure him of dying. She tells him she can only cure him of his murderous rage caused by the illness. 'Without that, I have no power.' 'You'll have the power of love.' Aiden finally lets his mother cure him. He comes out of it like the old Aiden. He spends quality time with Colleen and Molly. He tells Colleen there is one zombie alien ship left. All the living zombies will leave on it as soon as it's ready and return to their home world. He announces to the world that the zombie alien takeover is done, and he asks his followers to stand done. There is still some violence, but peace begins to take over the world again. Laws are passed all over the world: The zombie aliens and zombie alien human mixes are not welcome on Earth; they all must leave. Aiden grows ill, and he dies in his mother's arms. Again."

I begin to cry as I type. "Molly leaves to help get the ship ready. She comes to visit Colleen one last time before the ship leaves. They talk of Aiden. Colleen worries about Molly's life on a home world she's never seen. Molly assures her she'll be OK. 'I left you a present in the lab,' Molly tells her as she leaves. Not long after, Colleen watches the ship take off on TV. There are shots from all over the world of people cheering. The Earth is now zombie alien free."

"Now what?" Eartha asked. "Is that the end?"

Hayword laughed. "No!"

"What did Molly leave her?" David asked.

I continued typing and reading, "Colleen remembers then that Molly said she had left something for her in the lab. Colleen goes to the lab. She sees a large white basket on the floor. She hears whimpering. 'Oh no. I hope she didn't leave me a dog.' As she gets nearer, we see a baby blanket and then a baby girl. The baby gurgles. Colleen leans over and lifts the infant into the air. She can tell from her features that she's a little bit of Molly and a little bit of Aiden. Colleen smiles. And then the baby says very clearly, 'Hello, Grandma Colleen. Momma says it's whackadoo-dle time, and we better be ready to run. Are you ready to run?'

The camera moves out of the room and up and we see the words: The end.”

“Woot! Woot!” David said as they all clapped. “That’s great. I can’t wait to see it.”

“Good job, Mac.”

“Couldn’t have done it without you all,” I said.

“Yeah, you could have,” Hayword said.

“Give me a minute,” I said. I quickly read the treatment, and then I sent it to my phone, and then I sent it to Sally—and to Damon and Paolo for good measure. “OK. Done for now.”

“If we could all sit,” Eartha said. The few lights on inside the house were still dim. The electricity hadn’t come back on. Wind whistled around the house. I could hear distant and nearby thunder. I sat next to David. Hayword and Fern sat together. Eartha stayed standing.

“First, I’m so glad to be back here,” Eartha said. “Fern has given me permission to talk freely. Fern would like to start.”

“I want to apologize to my family,” Fern said. “I know I’m always bullshitting and lying. You have no reason to trust me. I will try to earn your trust. I’ve been acting crazy. I know. Mom, I really wasn’t thinking. To put alcohol in your drink to get you to act crazy is unforgivable. I was so high last week. I know that’s not an excuse, but it is a reason. It’s awful. This has been going on for a few months. And stealing the money. I am so sorry. I will pay it all back. I will do whatever I need to do. I’m sorry, Mom. I really didn’t mean to ruin your life or try to ruin your life. I just always figure you can bounce back.”

I nodded, but I was feeling very little. Except I didn’t trust her. But I didn’t feel as angry.

“I want to help make it right,” Fern said. “However I can.”

“You often apologize and then something happens and you do terrible or stupid things again,” Hayword said.

Wow. I couldn’t believe he was saying this. Finally.

"I think you need professional help," he said.

Fern nodded. "I do, too," she said. "I will go to rehab, and then Eartha has agreed to be my sober companion for a while. I intend to go into therapy."

"What's wrong with her?" David asked. "Why does she act this way?"

"You all experienced a trauma about fifteen years ago," Eartha said. "David got through it, probably because he was so young, and he was well taken care of through it all. Hayword and Brooke were adults. Fern was a pre-teen. She experienced her brother's death and then the house burned down and her mother spiraled into alcoholism. Trauma often causes children to kind of stop in time. Their emotional intelligence and maybe the brain itself is stuck in that time. That's what happened to Fern. In many ways, she is still a pre-teen."

Just like that, my anger melted away. I could see Fern in my mind's eye at that age, saw her wide tear-filled eyes back then. Looking at me. Wanting me to reassure her. I couldn't. I was too filled with grief. And so I left her there, stuck in that time when her baby brother stopped breathing.

"So her brain is broke?" David asked.

Fern laughed. "Yes, my brain is broke."

Hayword put his arm across Fern's shoulder. "Sorry, honey. You always seemed so tough. And you were always pushing us away, always saying you didn't need us."

"Of course," Fern said. "I was trying to convince myself I didn't need you all, I guess. I'm so tired."

I was glad Hayword could hold her, comfort her. I couldn't bring myself to go over to her.

Maybe I was just constitutionally unable to comfort another human being?

Or maybe just my children.

David leaned against me then. I put my arm across his shoulders, and he rested his head on my shoulder. Outside lightning lit up the early evening behind the curtain.

"It'll be OK, sweetheart," I whispered. "It'll be OK."

"I know," David said. "Because Fern will get well now."

I nodded. "Yes, yes, she will."

"Mom," Fern said, "do you think you can ever forgive me?"

"Um—"

CHAPTER NINETEEN

Just then the doorbell rang.

Thank god, because I didn't know how to answer Fern. Could I forgive her?

Rain was still pelting the windows. I glanced at Hayword, and then I got up, went to the door, and opened it. Joanie was standing on the other side of the door. She was soaking wet.

I shut the door again.

"Just the wind," I said as I came back to the living room.

The doorbell rang again.

"Goddamn it," I said. I went back and opened the door. "What?"

"My electricity is out," Joanie said. "Marv is haunting me. I keep hearing moaning."

"It's called the wind," I said.

Lightning flashed again and again.

"Please!" Joanie said.

I rolled my eyes, stepped aside, and swept my arm to let her know she could enter. Hayword, the kids, and Eartha gathered round.

"Joanie," Eartha said. "Long time."

The two women hugged. "You are soaked," Eartha said. "Let's get you a towel and dry you off."

I shrugged. Eartha was taking over just as she did the first time she came into our lives: I liked it. I did not want to deal with Joanie.

"Watch her every move!" I called as the two women went around the corner. Then I looked at my family. "Long story. OK, not that long. Marv is apparently sitting in his Jaguar in the back garage, dead. Joanie thinks he's haunting her."

David nodded. Fern laughed. "That's bizarre even for Joanie."

I thought it was too soon for Fern to be laughing.

Thunder rolled overhead again. Lightning flashed again and again. Fern moved closer to her brother.

"Is this how the world ends?" she asked.

"The world is ending all the time," I said.

Just then I heard my phone blip. I went into the living room and looked at it. Damon and Paolo both wrote on the thread that included Sally.

"The investors love the treatment," I said.

Sally wrote, too. "I like it, too. Good job."

I laughed and showed it to Hayword. "Like she means it. Oh, wait. She did a private text. 'Clever of you to show the boys. The script is still due.'"

I looked at Hayword.

"What are you waiting for?" he said. "Go write it. Use my office. A couple of the plugs work there when the generator is on."

I glanced over at my children who were now sitting on the

couch together talking quietly. I could hear Eartha and Joanie in the other room.

"No, I want to stay here. I can do it."

I began typing the script to the last *Beauty and the Zombie* movie. It felt bittersweet and perfect at the same time. The storm moved around the house like some uninvited guest doing everything it could to get inside. At some point, the five of them went into the kitchen to figure out what to eat. The fridge worked while the generator was on, but I didn't know what else. I didn't care. I closed my eyes and began writing.

They brought me salad and canned soup. Everyone chattered amiably around me. I didn't say much. I watched Fern. She seemed almost joyful. She had made promises: We would see if she kept them. I was rooting for her.

We opened the curtains at some point, turned off the lights, and watched the storm. The backyard was in light more often than dark: That was how often the lightning strikes were coming. I kept writing. I was dealing with a zombie alien invasion while sitting in our living room watching a lightning storm.

Then the doorbell rang.

"Oh my word," I said. "It's the worst storm in the century and we're getting more company than we've had in a century. I feel like I'm in a Joe Orton play."

This time Hayword answered the door. A moment later he returned to the living room with Philip Case.

This was puzzling.

"Well, hello, sailor," Joanie said.

I gave her a look as I stood. "Phil, nobody is supposed to be on the road. What are you doing here?"

"Can we go somewhere and talk?" Phil asked.

I looked at Hayword. "Let's go to my office."

Phil, Hayword, and I went upstairs to Hayword's office, closed the door, and sat around Hayword's desk.

"Did you tell her?" Phil asked.

"Tell me what?" I asked as Hayword shook his head.

"I asked Phil to do a deep dive into the Back to Life books," Hayword said.

"I know this genius forensic accountant who is very quick," Phil said. "I've hired her before."

"You could have called," I said. "It's dangerous out there."

"My son and his wife live in the village," he said. "I was checking on them, and I couldn't get a hold of either of you."

"Still," I said.

"Quit mothering him," Hayword said. "Let him talk."

"Fuck you," I said. "I wasn't mothering him. He's a friend. I was concerned."

"So you're friends now?" Hayword said. "I thought you didn't even like her."

"Ha!" I said. "I knew it."

"We've gotten to know each other better," Phil said.

"I know what that means," Hayword said.

"Fuck you," Phil said. "I wouldn't do that."

"No skin off my nose," Hayword said. "We're getting divorced."

"Could you both stop swinging your dicks around and tell me what you found," I said.

"Sally has embezzled $5,000,000 from the business in the last year," Phil said. "My guess is she has done this before because she barely covered her tracks. Most of the invoices go to On Location, a business that supposedly finds locations for movies. The business is registered to Sally McJames."

"And we haven't hired anyone to scout locations," Hayword said. "Certainly not for five million dollars."

I leaned back and laughed. "This is perfect."

"What? She stole five million dollars from us."

I nodded. "Yes. And that voids the contract. We can kick her out and take everything. She'll get nothing. We can throw her into jail."

"Embezzlement is often difficult to prove and prosecute," Phil said.

Maybe that meant Fern would be off the hook.

"You could negotiate with Sally to return the money," Phil said. "If she does that, you can tell her you won't prosecute."

"And then we split up the company and she still gets profits from the first two movies?" I said. "I don't like that."

"There are four funnel clouds!" I heard David cry from downstairs.

The three of us ran downstairs. David was looking at his pad. "Four funnel clouds in Los Angeles. They're heading this way. They are saying that everyone must stay indoors."

"They can't tell me what to do," Joanie said.

"Then go outdoors," I said. "Please."

I gazed at David's screen. The scene was like something out of a movie: downtown Los Angeles lit up by lightning and street lights that showed dark ominous tornados, like arms of a giant octopus looking for victims.

"Jesus," Phil said. "Do you have a basement?"

"No," Hayword said. "But we have a panic room. Would that protect us?"

Phil said, "I have no idea."

Eartha said, "Let's not panic."

"Hey, I was just gonna say that," I said.

"Go ahead," Eartha said.

I grinned. "No, you."

"Let's not panic," Eartha said. "Let's play some board games. We'll keep an eye on the news."

The six of them went to the kitchen table. I stayed in the living room and continued writing. I didn't care what Sally had done: I was going to follow the contract to the letter. And then I would squash her like a bug.

The storm battered the house for a long while. Then we experienced a brief lull. Suddenly I heard what sounded like squealing tires and breaking glass. I jumped up and ran toward the front door—along with everyone else in the full house. I swung the door open. Lightning flashed, and I saw a bloody man staggering toward us. It was dark again. And then lightning flashed, and the man's arms were stretched out toward us.

"Help!" he cried.

"Oh my god," I said. "It's Marv!"

I ran out into the pelting rain with Phil, Hayword, and Eartha beside me. Beyond Marv we could see a smashed car wedged up against one of our pine trees. We helped him inside and sat him at the kitchen table. Eartha got a cloth and gently wiped the blood off his forehead. Hayword got a bandage.

"I called 911," Phil said. "They can't get out here."

Where was Joanie? I looked behind me. She was cowering over by the fridge. "Is he real?" she whispered.

"Yes, he's real," I said. I put my hand on his arm. He looked a little dazed. "Should we take you to the hospital?"

"Where am I?" he asked.

"You're at Hayword's house," I said.

"Who is Hayword?"

"Christ, he's got dementia," Joanie said.

"Or amnesia."

"I am not demented," he said. "I just don't remember who I am or where I've been."

"He might have hit his head," Phil said. "We better take him to the local hospital."

"It's too dangerous," David said.

"Phil's a former cop," Hayword said. "He can take care of himself."

"I'll bring the car around," Phil said.

"I'll find a blanket for him," Eartha said.

"I'll get a drink," Joanie said.

The kids and Hayword disappeared with the rest of them, and I was alone with Marv. I rubbed his back. "It's OK," I said. "Phil will get you some help."

Marv looked at me. He winked. I squinted. Then I whispered, "Marv?"

"Yeah," he said. "I just couldn't figure out an excuse for why I'd been gone for a month. Figured amnesia could cover my ass for a while."

I laughed.

"Shhh," he said.

"She thinks you are dead in your Jaguar."

"What?" he asked.

"I went down there," I said. "Smelled like someone had died, looked like someone was in the driver's seat."

"I left my guitar there," he said. "I didn't want her touching it. She's always touching it. Probably a raccoon or something died in the garage."

"She thinks you've been haunting her."

He chuckled. "Serves her right."

"Where have you been?" I asked.

"In Mali, hunting," he said. "And other stuff. Wasn't ready to come home. She's always fucking around on me."

"You're too old to use that word," I said. "You look and sound like a dirty old man. A bloody dirty old man."

"Shhh, here they come."

Joanie patted her husband on the back. "I am so glad you're home, darling. I have been so worried. Amnesia. So Hollywood. Come on. Can you walk? Out to the car."

She helped Marv stand, and they headed out into the storm. Eartha came out with a blanket. "I'll go with them," she said.

"He's faking the amnesia," I said. "Don't you and Phil put your lives in danger for those two. They deserve each other."

"Thanks for telling me," Eartha said. She kissed my cheek. Then she called, "Fern, I will get in touch with you tomorrow. Stay sober! That goes for everyone."

Then she was gone. I leaned out the door. I could see Phil in the driver's seat. He saw me and waved. I smiled and waved, too. Then I flipped him off. He laughed. Off they drove.

David was beside me, watching. "What do you suppose that all meant? I mean in our life. Why did she think he was dead? Why did he turn up tonight of all nights? What does it mean?"

I looked at my son. "Nothing," I said. "It's just life. Most of life is absolutely meaningless."

We went back in the house and shut the door.

"That is depressing."

"It is meaningless until we give it meaning," I said. "Maybe Joanie was a toxic friend, and I needed to see it, truly. And I saw it. Truly. I am done with her."

The storm died down but did not end. I sat in the living room, writing. Fern and David said good night eventually and went to bed. David kissed me before he went upstairs. Fern kissed her father. She hesitated. I didn't encourage her, and she said goodnight and was gone. I looked up from the computer, and Hayword was gone, too.

I kept writing. Aiden came back to life. He was evil. He was cured of the disease. He was good. And then he died in his mother's arms. Again. The end.

I sent the script to Sally, Paolo, and Damon.

I felt drained. That was fast even for me.

I opened the curtains. It was almost morning. The clouds were gray. The rain was light.

I went upstairs and looked into David's room. He was sleeping. I tiptoed to his bed and kissed the top of his head. "I love you," I said.

Then I went to Fern's room. I could hear her sleep breathing. She looked so small. I went to her bed and looked down. I remembered when she was born. She had screamed like she was pissed at the world for being dragged from my womb. I had loved her so much. I wanted only good things for her. I bit my lip. Now I wanted to crawl into bed with her and tell her everything would be all right. I put my hand on her hair. "Of course I forgive you," I whispered. "I will love you always and forever." I kissed the top of her head.

I went into Hayword's room. He was sprawled all over the bed. I guess he had finally gotten used to sleeping without me. When we were together, he always left a place for me in bed. He looked younger now, as he slept. As if all the cares in the world were gone. I smiled. I felt . . . I felt . . . I felt all the love in the world wash over me as I watched him. Love for him, for the kids, for our life together. I backed out of the room and went downstairs to the living room.

I opened the sliding glass door and went outside. I walked across the grass in my bare feet. Except for a few downed branches, it looked like the house and environs had done OK. We had survived the worst lightning storm in the Earth's history—as far as we knew—unscathed. I sank to the wet ground. This was where we had spread Alberto's ashes. This was his grave.

It started to rain again, hard, and I began to sob. I had loved Alberto so much. And he died. I loved Hayword. He had disappointed me. I loved Fern, and she behaved badly. I loved David, and he was filled with anxiety. I loved them all and like Alberto, they would all die. We would all die. We would fail each other, and we would die.

I had spent the last fifteen years holding them all at arm's length. I had spent all that time holding grudges because they had failed me or worried me and because I knew it was safer to be away from them.

The truth was I loved them. I missed them. I missed Alberto.

I curled up on the wet grass and wept. The rain stopped, and I fell asleep.

Then Alberto was there. He was a young man, a handsome young man, a cross between me and Hayword and Ryan. He leaned down and held his hand out. I took it, and he gently pulled me up.

"Hello, Mom," he said.

"Hello, sweetheart," I said.

We put our arms around each other and held each other tightly. I could feel his body so warm and firm and alive.

"I miss you," I said.

"But they're all still here," he said. "You need them."

"Look, there's a rainbow," I said. "The storm must be over."

He kept his arm around my waist. "Remember, there's no place like home." He pointed to his chest and then to mine.

"Are you saying home is where the heart is?" I asked.

He nodded. I laughed. "So you would have grown up to be a cornball," I said. "Love does not fix everything. I loved you, and you still died."

"That's true," he said, "but bitterness fixes nothing. Tell everyone I said hello."

He kissed my forehead.

I opened my eyes. Hayword was kissing the top of my head. Next to him were Fern and David. "She's awake," one of them said. I smiled, and then I began to cry. And they all started crying. We hugged each other, sitting on the wet grass, and we cried.

"What are you all crying about?" I asked.

"I dunno," David said. "You started it."

Then we all laughed and fell back on the grass.

"By the way," Hayword said, "everyone got home OK. Marv is fine. And Damon and Paolo love the script."

"I don't care what they think," I said. "As long as you liked it, as long as you all liked it. The rest of them can go fuck themselves."

"I thought it was the best one yet," Hayword said.

"I liked the little girl in the end," Fern said. "I think you should call her Fern."

"You know she's a half-alien zombie," David said.

Fern shrugged. "Takes one to know one."

CHAPTER TWENTY

Eventually we let each other go, and we came into the house. I was soaked through. Needed a shower. I looked at my phone first. I read Damon and Paolo's texts about how fabulous the script was. "Perfection!" Sally was silent on the subject. Didn't matter. I had fulfilled my contract. There was a text message from Katherine Bernstein. She said, "We are sorry, but we can't do what you ask. Sally is not our kind of people. But you are. Call us."

"Hey, David," I called. "Don't go to school this morning."

"Why?"

"I want to take you somewhere," I said. "You and Fern and your dad. Have him call the school."

The three of them were picking up debris when I came out of the shower and got dressed. I heard Hayword say something about the lightning rod going to good use last night. Then I sat on the bed and called Katherine.

"Hello, darlin'," Katherine said. "How'd you fare last night?"

"We did fine," I said. "You?"

"A few lightning struck trees," Katherine said. "They are now works of art. We are fine. I am sorry to disappoint you about Sally."

"I'm not disappointed at all," I said. "In fact, I would have had to call and tell you some things I found out about her if you were going to offer her the job."

"We would like to sell OK Studios to you and Hayword," Katherine said. "Our entire catalog and this place."

I was stunned. Shocked. Flabbergasted.

"We could see how much you enjoyed the place," she said, "and it only seems right since your story started it. It's time for us to be with our grandchildren and put some of our money to good use. We'll give you a good and fair price, one you can afford. If you're interested."

"I don't know what to say. You've made me speechless. Don't tell anyone; they'll want to know how you did it. Let me talk to Hayword. In fact, can I bring him and the kids to your place today and show them around?"

"Of course!" Katherine said. "We have to go into the city, but come anyway. I'll leave the key under the mat."

"OK, thank you."

Then I went outside and asked Hayword if he was ready to go talk to Sally.

"Let me make a couple of phone calls first," Hayword said. "I want to keep Damon and Paolo on board to help us make the third film."

I nodded.

I helped the kids pick up.

"How are you feeling today?" I asked Fern.

"Good," she said. "Better than I have in a long while. I think I can do this."

"We'll be here for you," I said.

Hayword soon returned. "Damon and Paolo are in. They'll keep quiet. Called Caryn. Sally is at the offices."

"OK, kids," I said. "We have to stop at the office first, and then I want to take you all somewhere."

On the way in to the office, I called our lawyer Mercy and told her what was happening. I asked her to get the dissolution papers drawn up and send them to us ASAP. I wanted Sally to sign them today.

Phil was waiting outside the offices. I glanced at Hayword. "He's our muscle," Hayword said. I was nervous, but I laughed. Phil kissed me on the cheek.

"I'm security," he said. "When companies fire someone, they often have them escorted out of the building."

I nodded. "OK. Let's do this thing."

I stopped at the desk and said hello to Caryn.

"Caryn, I need you to call a locksmith and get all of the locks changed today," I said. "And get Sally off of any accounts she may have and deactivate any accounts she has, including email."

"What's going on?" Caryn asked.

"She stole five million dollars from us," I said, "so her ass is being fired."

Caryn's eyes widened, but she nodded. "I'll get it done."

Sally looked superior as hell when we came into her office. Then I said, "We know you embezzled five million dollars from the company."

She didn't deny it. "Those were legitimate expenses."

I laughed.

"I will sell all of the photos to the tabloids," she said, "if you don't let bygones be bygones."

"I don't care about the fucking photos," I said. "You called my daughter a slut. You stole from me. You threatened me. We are so over you."

Hayword said, "You violated the contract. It is against the law to embezzle and to blackmail. Our contract with you is now null and void."

"We won't go to the police or the press about this as long as you go quietly," I said. "You will relinquish all shares you have in this company. And we will owe you nothing."

"But *Part Three* will make millions."

"So?" I said. "You made no contribution to it."

"Give me a week to get things in order," she said.

"You mean to get your story straight," I said. "No. You are gone within the hour. Phil Case here will make certain of it. We'll have the papers sent to your house for you to sign today."

She didn't put up much of a fight. Maybe she was ready. Maybe she was done. Or she knew she could go to jail.

"I'm sorry it's come to this," I told her. "I thought we were friends."

"Guess you were wrong," she said. "You were always a lousy fuck anyway."

"I beg to differ," Hayword said.

I chuckled. Then I said, "Phil, she's all yours. Make sure she doesn't download anything or take anything with her, including keys to the place."

Phil stepped into the room, and we stepped out.

And Sally St. James was gone from my life.

It was a beautiful ride to the OK Studios. Fern and David talked with each other in the back seat, sometimes laughing, sometimes serious. They didn't know where we were going. I just told Hayword that Katherine and Oscar invited us out to their place. I didn't tell him anything else.

"In the middle of all this you want to go spend a day in the country?" he asked me.

"Yes."

And then we were there. Hayword parked the car, and we all got out. Fern and David ran away from the house, down a dirt road that led up over the hill, just like they would have done if they were still kids. Hayword and I stood looking around, and then we walked slowly toward the house.

"I had forgotten how beautiful it is out here," he said. "Wow."

We stood in the shade of the porch, near the table and chairs where I'd sat yesterday. Then I went to the door, retrieved the key from under the mat, and then unlocked the door.

"Wait!" Hayword said. "What are you doing?"

"Katherine told me where the key was," I said. I opened the door and motioned him inside. I closed the door, took his hand, and led him to the courtyard. We stood amongst the thousands of colorful flowers. Bees buzzed all around us.

"What's going on, Mac?" Hayword asked. He looked at the wooden table: *There's no place like home.*

"Katherine and Oscar are retiring as you know" I said. "And they want to sell the studio, this house, and all the property to us. The entire catalog. *Love and Other Insanities* would be ours. All the small beautiful movies they've made would be ours. They are the kind of movies we've always wanted to make. And now we could make more of them. I even have an idea for a sequel, twenty years later. *Love and Other Sanities.* Or maybe even a TV series."

"They are selling? Can we afford it?"

"She says we could," I said. "Hayword, thirty some years ago, we got together and envisioned a life for ourselves. We wanted to tell stories and do good. And then things went whack-adoodle. My brain got stuck on Alberto's death and my unhappiness. But I know what I want now."

Hayword looked around. "This? This is what you want? It is amazing."

I laughed. "No, well, yes, but no. I want you. I do love you. I loved our life. I want to be close to you and close to the children. But new. I want us to be our best selves together."

Hayword looked down at me. "I can't promise to be my best self."

"Quit making me laugh," I said. "You said you wanted a divorce. That's fine. I don't want to be your wifey or you be the husband. I want us to be together because we've built a life together, because we like each other, because we love each other. Home is where the heart is and my heart is with you and the kids." I took his hand.

"That is really corny," he said. "Sounds like something I would say."

"Alberto gave me the line," I said.

Hayword smiled.

"We could do the work we want to do here," I said.

He looked around. He squeezed my hand. "You had me at 'Hayword.'"

I slugged him. He leaned down and kissed me.

"What about all of your boyfriends and all the great sex you'll be missing?" he asked.

"They are all such prima donnas," I said, "and I'm good with mediocre sex."

"Hey," he said. "Man, this could be fun."

"That's the idea."

We heard the kids calling us. I phoned David and told him to come in the front door and gave him directions to the courtyard. When they saw the flowers, they both gasped.

"Oh Mom," Fern said. "I want to live here forever."

"Well, maybe not forever," I said, "but your dad and I are buying it. At least we hope so."

"You and Dad?" David said. "Are you back together? Like a couple?"

Hayword looked at me. I said, "Yes. We're all in."

"Who is going to tell Patricia?" David asked.

"You were so fond of her," I said, "so you can do it."

It was a busy couple of years. We bought OK Studios and moved into the place within two months. Katherine and Oscar bought my bungalow to be closer to their family. We rented out the house. Since Alberto's ashes were there, we didn't want to sell it. We found a nice young family who were a little strapped for cash and gave them a good deal on rent.

Back to Life Studios became a division of OK Studios, more as a bookkeeping thing then anything else. We closed the offices in Los Angeles. We hired Caryn for OK Studios, and she came to live in one of the guest houses with her wife, Cameron.

We dissolved The Alberto Foundation. We split the money between the kids and told them to do with it what they would, but that was the end of it. They had to make their own way in the world.

Fern went to rehab. (I got clean and sober, too.) She came home and lived in one of the guest houses with Eartha. It was a rough time. Fern can be vicious as hell. As her brain began to heal from years of drugs and alcohol, she became kinder and more compassionate. Damon still had a crush on her. He came around more and more. They began dating.

We put *Beauty and the Zombie Part Three* on hold for six months. Fortunately everyone was able to move their schedules around. The shoot went off perfectly.

Joanie is no longer a part of my life. Neither is Sally, obviously. I don't miss them. I miss Mark now and again. I don't see Ryan at all. I called him early on and apologized for my part in his relapse. We talk now and again, just to see how the other one is doing.

Hayword and I understand how fortunate we are. We are working on ways to give back. A portion of our profits is going to organizations that are combating climate change. We care for our land sustainably—and it's a constant learning experience.

I am happy. I feel like I've finally found home. I don't know if it will last. I am nervous to say it out loud. I enjoy my husband. Yes, we never bothered with the divorce. We work hard not to fall back into old patterns. We love the house and the land. We love OK Studios. We see Katherine and Oscar often.

One night a few weeks before the premiere of *Beauty and the Zombie Part Three,* Hayword, David, Fern, Damon, and I sat on the front porch looking up at the night sky after a special dinner to celebrate David graduating from high school.

Fern said, "I have an announcement."

"You're getting married?" David said.

"No!" Fern said. "Why would I participate in that patriarchal bullshit?"

"That's my girl," I said.

"Phil and Eartha are dating," she said.

"You mean you have gossip," David said.

Fern shrugged.

"Fern, I always forgot to ask you about the handbags," I said. "Why were they filled with liquor bottles?"

"It was a selling point," Fern said. "I figured it was the end of the world and everyone should stock up on booze."

I laughed. "That makes absolutely no sense."

"I agree," Fern said. "But you know what, everyone who bought a bag was so excited when they opened them up and saw the tiny liquor bottles."

"I have no idea what you all are talking about," Damon said.

"Oops," Fern said. "I may have forgotten to tell you about the handbags."

We all laughed.

"Do you think Alberto is alive somewhere?" Fern asked. "Do you think he watches us and roots for us and knows we're finally doing all right?"

"I don't know," I said. I looked at Hayword. He shrugged.

"I have no wise words on the subject," he said.

"I say if we see a falling star in the next minute or so, that means yes," David said. "Alberto is alive somewhere and he watches over us."

We all looked more intently at the sky.

Nothing.

Nothing.

Please give him this, I whispered.

Nothing.

Then a star streaked across the sky.

We all cheered.

"He's alive," David said. "Does that mean my brother is a zombie?"

"No!" Fern said. "I say if we see another star right away, it means that Alberto is happy that we're happy."

We stared.

Nothing.

Nothing.

No…

A star streaked across the sky. And then another one fell. And another. We counted ten falling stars. I made wish after wish for happiness and good health for my children.

We laughed. Cried a little bit. Were amazed.

It could have been that we went through a meteor shower. Maybe it was that time of year. I wasn't going to look. David didn't even look. In that moment, we let the mystery be.

"We love you, Alberto!" Fern called.

"We love you, Alberto!" David said.

We all stood and raised our glasses to the sky, and we cried, "We love you, Alberto!" to the night.

"Rest in peace," I added.

That is my story, and I'm sticking to it.

Kim Antieau's novels include Brooke McMurphy's first two adventures, *Whackadoodle Times* and *Whackadoodle Times Two,* as well as *The Jigsaw Woman, Her Frozen Wild, Church of the Old Mermaids, Coyote Cowgirl, The Monster's Daughter, Butch, Killing Beauty,* and many others. Learn more at www.kimantieau.com.